D1522114

SCANDALOUS

www.SexyAwesomeBooks.com

SCANDALOUS

H.M. Ward

Laree Bailey Press

SCANDALOUS

CHAPTER ONE

Rain splattered on the windshield of the cab in globs. Each splash sounded like a rock. I was used to nasty storms from living in Texas for so long, but it made the people who never left New York cringe. The cabbie was an oversized man with pasty skin and too much hair. He had a dark ball cap pulled down low, concealing his face. As we drove into the storm, he pushed his hat farther back, as if ball caps hindered vision. The man was leaning forward, practically pressing his face against the windshield.

We drove east in silence. He didn't try to make small talk, and I was glad about that. This homecoming wasn't something I wanted to discuss. I still didn't want to be here, but there was nowhere left to go. The car pulled off the expressway, and after a few turns, the cab rolled down a narrow street in Port Jeff. Through the rain, porch lights blazed promising warmth inside the rows of homes.

"Here we are," the cabbie stated with complete indifference. As he told me the total, he wrote something on a clipboard, and tossed it back onto the front seat next to him.

Hesitating for a moment, I looked up at the brown brick facade and swallowed. Maybe this wasn't a good idea. I'd left Long Island over ten years ago, and, although I missed it, I had never wanted to come back. Yet, here I was.

The cabbie cleared his throat, waiting. I blinked once, pushing away the doubt that crawled up my spine, and dug into my purse. It pained me to hand him the last of my money, but I did. He grumbled something, expecting me to be cheap because I looked like a drowned rat, but I said, "Keep the change."

"Sure thing, Princess. I'll buy a new yacht to park next to the other one." The man laughed. He sounded like a llama choking on a shoe. Fine. It wasn't a big tip, but it was all I had. I got the clear impression he didn't think Little Miss Texas should be wandering around big bad New York, like some redneck yokel who just discovered shoes.

Ignoring him, I slid off the seat. Kicking open the door, rain splattered down and I was instantly wetter. I didn't think that was possible. I had one bag with me and two others in the trunk. Drops of freezing rain ran down my neck and into my coat making me shiver. I'd forgotten how different men acted here. They didn't hold doors or help girls with their bags. After I ran around to the back of the cab, I grabbed my suitcases and slammed the trunk shut.

As the red taillights faded into the darkness, the front door of 6A opened. A young woman with long dark hair ran down the porch stairs and straight at me. "Abby!" In two bounds she was across the puddles, hugging me like I'd never left.

"Hey, Kate," I hugged her back. She didn't seem to care that I was sopping wet, and now, so was she. Holding my shoulders in her hands, she examined me under the street light. Her eyes were still vibrant, and every ounce as green as I remembered.

"I can't believe it's been so long since I've seen you," Kate said grinning, shaking her head. "I have no idea why you ran away and failed to tell your best friend about it, but I would have traded anything to get to see you again. And now you're here!" She hugged me again. I wasn't much of a hugger, and neither was she, but she was right. With the way I'd left, I didn't expect such a warm reception. "Come on, let's go inside. I have a spiked hot cocoa with your name on it." She reached for my bags, and then made a beeline for the front door with me on her heels.

———

Kate didn't know why I'd left, and I never told her. It was complicated. As I stepped over the threshold, I glanced around her apartment. It was warm and clean, decorated like an art gallery with beautiful artwork on the walls. The room was peaceful, painted with soft blues and browns—not like the girl with the bright orange bedroom she had when we were younger. Kate seemed to have gotten over her fascination with neon colors.

Pushing her dripping hair out of her face, Kate said, "Come on. I'll show you your room, and then we can catch up." Following Kate's path of puddles, I walked between the living room and kitchen to a back hallway. The apartment was larger than it appeared from the street. After passing a bathroom, I stopped in the doorway of a bedroom. Kate grabbed my bags from me, putting them under a window and throwing towels on the floor in front of them to soak up the water. "And this, Miss Abigail Tyndale, will be your residence for as long as you like."

"It'll only be a year, Kate. I'll go as soon as I can. I don't want to burden you." I felt horrible having to do this in the first place, and she was being so nice. Kate was the same selfless person from a decade ago. I bet she still dragged half dead cats off the street and took them to the vet, happily footing their medical bills and finding them a new home.

Kate folded her arms over her chest, and hung her head. "You're gonna run again, aren't you? First chance you get, you'll head for the hills and go back to no-mans land." It was a statement. An obvious observation. A dark tendril of hair clung to Kate's cheek, water dripping down her face like tears. Her green eyes were on me, wanting an answer.

No one willingly ran to no-mans land. I sure didn't and standing there with her, it felt like I'd never left. It felt like I had my best friend back, and I missed her. No one took her place in all the time I was gone. She was the kind of person who didn't say what you wanted to hear—she said what you needed to hear. Friends like her were rare.

I smiled at her, "This isn't my home anymore. I don't belong here." My moist clothing clung to me like wet toilet paper. I repressed a shiver. A hot shower really sounded divine.

"You belong with your family," she stated, stubbornly.

I wondered if she'd heard—if she knew. One night, several years ago, my parents were driving back from dinner and never got home. They were hit, head on, by a car going 90 miles per hour. Everything shattered. There was nothing left. No chance for survival. No chance to say good-bye. "They're all dead, Kate. I'm alone," I said softly staring at her.

She smiled sadly at me, "I know Abby, but that wasn't what I meant. Your friends are your family now. You're not alone, unless you choose to be." As she left my room, she said over her shoulder, "It's time to stop running."

CHAPTER TWO

The door clicked shut. There was truth in her words, truth that I didn't want to hear. After a hot shower, I donned a pair of sweats and headed out to the living room. The plastic soles of my slippers made me sound like a water-buffalo traipsing through the apartment. The wooden floors didn't conceal much noise, although the dark wood looked nice.

Kate was in the kitchen, standing by the stove, with a kettle in her hand. She beamed when she saw me. "Choose your poison, cinnamon schnapps or something stronger?" Kate had changed her water-logged clothing too and was wearing a pair of boxers and a tank top. Her damp hair was pulled back into a pony tail.

Sitting on the couch, I pulled my legs in tight. "No schnapps, Kate. Just plain cocoa."

She arched an eyebrow at me, the bottle pausing before she poured it into my cup. "Seriously? No alcohol?"

I nodded. "Part of the vows—alcohol is only used in rituals." If Kate's eyebrows climbed any higher, they'd be in her ponytail. I laughed, "I'm fine, Kate. It doesn't have to be spiked."

"It should be," she mumbled, carrying over two oversized cups. Handing me one, she sat down across from the sofa on a large suede chair. After taking a sip she asked, "So, this must be rough." I nodded once, not meeting her eyes. "How long were you working there?"

I sipped my drink, not looking up, "Since I started seminary, so twelve years or so." The mug felt warm against my hands. I wished she'd talk about something else, but my mind was drawing a blank. It was like I couldn't think of a single thing to derail her questions.

"What was your job?" she asked carefully.

"Preacher. Minister. The normal churchy kind of stuff." Taking another sip, I looked up at her. I knew what she wanted to ask me, but I didn't want to talk about it. Not yet, anyway.

Her legs were pulled sideways, mirroring mine. She was leaning on her left arm, steaming mug in her right hand. "That sounds nice." She was trying to be sweet. Nice was the last word for what it was. If Dante had a version of Hell with pictograms, I think the gun-wielding cow folk would have been around level four. At first I adored them, like crazy old coots, but the longer I was there the more I saw that they thought I was the nutty one. I nodded again. Kate looked at her mug and blurted out the dreaded question. "So what'd you do?"

Kate's green eyes were wide, a grin on her face. "I have to ask. It's killing me, Abby. For the past decade I'm lucky if I've heard from you twice. And then all of a sudden you get tossed on your ass—by a church! Did you curse them out from the pulpit? Or what?"

I cringed. "Maybe." She knew I had issues controlling my tongue. Before I headed south and signed on the clergy dotted line, I swore like a sailor. Spewing profanity from the pulpit was a normal occurrence for me, although the words they blanched at were words like 'crap' and 'hell.' Really, Hell is a noun. They should have gotten over that, but that wasn't what got me banished. I hedged, "Kate, I really don't want to rehash it. I did something bad—something that should have gotten me fired—but they said that they'd keep me if I took a mandatory sabbatical." There it was. The statement I practiced on the plane flying up here.

"So a year of vacation—that's not that bad, right?" she sipped from her mug, green eyes peering at me.

I laughed, trying to defuse the tension I felt building in my shoulders. I was mad, angry. This wasn't fair, but it's the way things were. I had to deal with it. I said, "If that's what they did, it would have been fine. But they didn't." I hesitated. Talking about this just made me more emotional. I walked into this mess. I brought it on myself and now I was homeless. I decided to tell her more. It was Kate, and I doubt she'd condemn me for what I did, although I wouldn't specify exactly what—not yet. "The church board said it was a year in the desert—they wouldn't pay my salary—and that if I wanted to remain employed, that I had to do this."

"So, basically you were tossed out on your ass with no money?" Kate's expression was surprised. "That doesn't sound like a churchy thing for them to do."

I nodded, "Yeah, but it's actually much worse." My stomach sank. This was the kicker and it was my own damn fault.

"How could it possibly be worse?" her jaw was hanging open, her mug tilted precariously to the side, its contents threatening to spill onto the floor. To Kate, bad was a finding a mugger in the bathroom stall, and what I was about to tell her would set her on full attack. I just hoped I wouldn't get blasted when I told her how stupid I was. This was the biggest mistake I ever made, aside from getting almost-fired.

Avoiding her gaze, I explained, "They hired me while I was in college. I was working on a ministry degree and I could have been an assistant minster somewhere, maybe with youth or something. But this church wanted me as their one and only minister. They wanted me to do seminary. It was three years of grad work on top of the student loans I already had. I said I couldn't afford it, but we reached an agreement..."

Kate groaned, "Oh no. Tell me you didn't."

My throat tightened. I stared into my cocoa. I was stupid. While most kids had some debt from school that followed them around like a puppy, stealing their meager wages, making it harder to survive, I had a freaking walrus. It sat on me, it squashed me, and made my life a living hell. I thought Kate's parents were deranged lunatics. They were anti-credit card. I can't imagine the bitch-slap her mom would give me if I admitted to my walrus-sized loans.

Pressing my lips together, I nodded, "I did. I took out more loans to pay for grad school. The way my contract with the church was worded, it said that they would pay off my debt as part of my salary." It didn't seem like a bad idea at the time, and I really didn't know the difference between ten dollars and ten grand. Apparently the lenders know that stuff. So did the church board.

Kate closed her eyes, shaking her head, immediately catching on, "And since they aren't giving you a salary for this entire year..."

"I have to repay my astronomical student loans on my own." I ran my fingers through my hair, practically pulling it out. There were so many major mistakes, and they were all super-sized. "I don't know what to do, Kate. The church provided the parsonage. They gave me enough money to pay my bills and eat. It wasn't enough to save anything. I was lucky that I had enough money to get here. When I told them that, they said the lilies of the field don't worry about tomorrow and neither should I. What am I supposed to? If you hadn't taken me in, I'd have nowhere to go."

They screwed me. My church, the people I dedicated my life to, completely and totally screwed me. They wrote this off as a learning experience that would make me stronger. They broke their word about making sure my loans were paid every month without a second thought. Fury flamed to life inside of me. My fingers ran through my hair as that nauseating sense of desperation crawled up my throat again. It felt like I was being choked, but nothing was there. Hanging my head, I pressed my eyes closed, fighting to hold back the tears that were building behind my eyes.

Kate tapped the side of her cup, thinking, "Okay, let's not freak out, yet. We need to address the loans first. You have a place to stay and you don't have to worry about food, either." She grinned, "I'm an awesome cook. No more Spaghetti-os for you!" Glancing up at her, head in my hands, I couldn't find the smile within me. I felt crushed, like some huge ogre stepped on me, smashing me flat. "Okay, let's see. I didn't do the loan thing. My parents thought debt was the devil's doing. But loan companies have options in case of emergencies, deferments to make repayment easier if there's a crisis. Abby, have you filed for a deferment? I bet you could claim financial hardship and they'd give you a year or more before demanding another payment."

I shook my head, "I don't have anymore. We used them all."

"We?" she asked, her mouth gaping like a fish.

I cringed. It sounded utterly stupid now that I was explaining it to someone else. Sitting back in my chair, I looked up at her. "The board. They asked me to use all my deferments before they began repayment. I didn't think they'd toss me, so I used them… Oh my God, Kate." My eyes were wide. I didn't see how screwed I was until right then. Before saying it out loud, it had been an abstract thought of screwed-ness, drifting aimlessly through my mind. But now that I'd said it, it solidified and fell to my toes like a lead pancake.

Kate leaned forward, putting her mug down, her game face on. "The past is the past, Abby. You can't change it. The only thing to do is try and come up with enough money to pay it. It can't be that much,

~ 14 ~

right? What is it? A couple hundred bucks a month? That's doable. A minimum wage job would do that— you could work part-time and you'll be totally fine."

I shook my head and a tangle of reddish brown hair tumbled forward, freeing itself from my ponytail. "It's $3275 per month." I tucked the wayward strands behind my ear, saying the number completely numb. It was so astronomical that I should have been a doctor.

Kate's jaw dropped so wide that I could see every tooth in her head. "Holy fuck! How much do you owe?"

"Just over $270,000." Kate sat there stunned, recognizing the walrus. I sat there like the dumb-ass that I was, shaking my head, pressing my finger tips to my temples. "I need a job. I need a good job, fast." If I kept saying it, maybe I wouldn't freak out.

Kate came to her senses. She blinked those bright green eyes, as she shook the shock away, "Abby, what's mine is yours. I'll help you as much as I can. Don't worry about rent or groceries. I'll take care of that for a while." She shook her head, "Damn, that's a lot of debt. You need at least four grand to pay that, otherwise you won't have enough money after taxes. The market sucks here right now. And your degree doesn't help you."

"I know. I tried to find work in Texas, before I left, but even down there in God's country I'm useless. No one wants a minister around when they aren't at church." They told me some crap about not wanting God looking over their shoulders at work. That stuff was for Sunday, as if they could lock God in the church building.

Kate frowned, "What else have you done since high school?" I didn't answer. My brain reached back trying to think of something unrelated to my ministry degrees. Kate straightened in her seat, an idea spreading across her face, "Ooh! What about art? Tell me you took some college art classes." Before I could answer she bounded down the hallway and came back holding a newspaper. She flicked through the pages.

"Yeah," I said slowly, watching her flip through the thin newsprint, "I took some art history, photography, and a painting class—but they were all electives with an emphasis on religious art."

She snorted, "Of course they were," she glared at me from over the top of the paper, "but you aren't going to tell anyone else that, unless they ask. Got it? Besides, most early art was religious anyway. It won't matter."

"Kate," I began to protest, but stopped when she slammed the paper down in front of me. Her narrow finger pointed toward an article that said LOCAL MUESUM OPENS SOON. I stared at the paper, but couldn't fathom what she was suggesting. "Clue me in, Kate. What are you thinking?"

"Well, a few weeks ago someone called MOMA looking for a new curator, and it was this place!" She pointed to the paper again. "I was the one who took the call. Abby, they're brand new, so they can't afford a seasoned professional—they need someone like you. Odds are it'll pay your loans and maybe give you a little pocket change. In other words, it's a crap job that no one can live off of unless they have an awesome roommate like me!" She beamed. "Plus, a reference from MOMA can't hurt. I'll call her first thing tomorrow." For the first time in days, I smiled and laughed. Maybe things would work out after all.

CHAPTER THREE

Or maybe not.

My heart sank, clunking into the bottom of my shoes as the dreaded words poured out of the woman's mouth, "The position has been filled." The girl at the desk informed me before I even finished saying my name. The vastness of the empty room seemed to make her voice louder. "It was earlier today, actually. I'm sorry, dear. I tried to get hold of you, but there was no cell number."

My shoulders slumped slightly, though I tried to hide it. Kate had spent the morning on the phone to get me this interview. There was no way I could afford a cell phone, so I didn't have one. Apparently Kate's recommendation wasn't enough to overcome the preacher thing. I smiled softly at her, "Thank you for trying. I really appreciate it."

As I turned to leave, she called out, "Hon!" I stopped and turned back to face her. She was scrawling something on a notepad. The museum was closed, so she was wearing jeans and a tee shirt. Plaster was splattered across her lap. "Wait!" I stopped, as she crossed the room quickly. "Listen, I heard that the Galleria needs help. It's not a museum, but it's an art job.

"The Galleria?" I asked, looking at the paper she handed me.

"Yeah, it's not too far from here. It's on the south shore in the Hamptons. Some rich guy owns it. That job'll get snapped up fast. If I were you, I'd head over there right now." She smiled at me. Her kindness floored me. I stood there for a moment before I found my voice.

"Thank you. Thank you so much!" I looked at the address as I slipped back inside Kate's car. She worked at the Museum of Modern Art, otherwise known as MOMA, and said I could use her car. She worked crazy hours and said she wouldn't miss it.

The maps of Long Island that I had in my head were old, but I thought I knew where the address that the woman handed me was located. I didn't have a cell phone, and Kate's car was too old to have GPS. I looked at the address again, wondering if I should go—if I could pull off a job interview when I didn't even know what the job was. I was flying by the seat of my pants and hating every moment of it.

That choking sensation climbed out of my belly again, threatening my sanity. Without a job I'd lose everything I worked so hard on for the past ten years. My credit would be trashed, student loan collectors would harass me to no end, and my contract with the church would be violated. I didn't think anything of it at the time, requiring a person to keep their credit in good standing seemed like a reasonable part of a job. However, since they were the ones that caused the financial distress, it hardly seemed fair now.

Glancing in the rearview mirror, I pulled out. How hard would it be to fake my way through an interview? Anyway, I was already dressed. No point in giving up, not yet. Where there's a will, there's a way—and other crap like that sputtered through my mind. What was the worst that could happen? Without hesitation, I drove directly to the address on the paper. My jaw nearly fell off my face when I pulled up. It was a large studio and art gallery—and it was beachfront property—on the most expensive part of Long Island. The official name was Jonathan Gray Fine Art & Galleria. It was in carved golden letters on a blue sign in front of the door.

Stepping from my car, I hurried up the front walk, noticing the white sand. The sound of the ocean crashing into the shore filled my ears. When I pulled open the door, several women who were dressed far better than me sat waiting in a poshly decorated room. Confidently, I walked to the desk, although I felt lacking when I saw the other women's clothing. Their skirts and blouses hugged their bodies as if the garments were custom made. I was wearing my Texas Target dress with a white collared shirt underneath. Holy crap. I looked like a Sunday School teacher, or a nun in her street clothes. These were the wrong clothes for a place like this, but it was too late to do anything about it now.

The receptionist smiled wanly at me and handed me a clipboard. "You're late," she scolded. "I shouldn't even let you in, but since they haven't started the first round yet, I'll make an exception. Fill out your paperwork quickly. Mr. Gray doesn't have all day."

I nodded, smiling, and sat down next to a breathing Barbie doll. She arched a perfectly plucked brow at me, no doubt questioning my black frock and clunky shoes. Ignoring her, I filled out my paperwork. My heart raced a little bit. I didn't realize how much I wanted this, but I did. I missed doing creative things; I missed the challenge of it. And the job description plastered across the top of the papers made me giddy. I would be a gallery assistant. The salary was stated with an additional commission on each sale. I'd easily be able to pay my loans on time, and not mooch off of Kate. Hope swelled in my chest.

It took two hours for them to call my name. I was the last candidate. I followed the receptionist into a large room. There were several floor-to-ceiling windows that overlooked the ocean. My eyes went straight to the windows, staring at the sea. I didn't realize how much I missed it.

"Miss Tyndale," a man's voice called me back to reality. He held out a chair for me before moving around the long empty table to the other side. "I'm

Gus Peck. I'll be conducting your interview. As you know we are a prestigious art studio. Jonathan Gray's works sell for a premium to affluent clientele. Are you comfortable working with the wealthy?"

Smiling, I leaned forward, "Yes. I've worked with many different people in the past. Some were difficult, but that was only because they demanded the best. Other personalities may have seemed easier to deal with at first, but they proved harder to assist." Was that a good answer? Interviewing for church jobs was very different. There was a fine line between telling them what they wanted to hear and what I really thought. Everyone was on best behavior, asking questions that usually didn't matter, but Gus' question seemed rather practical. It threw my footing off a little bit, as did his reply.

"How's that?" Gus asked, jotting down things on a yellow notepad as I spoke, his eyes not lifting to meet mine.

How is that, Abby? I was totally making stuff up, pulling answers out of the air on the fly. Explaining my rationale, I replied, "Well, the difficult people came across that way because they were demanding, but demanding people know what they want. They have clear expectations and expect them to be met." Gus stopped scribbling and looked up at me as I continued, "It can be intimidating if you haven't dealt with them before. But the easy-going people are actually harder to help, because they usually don't know what they need. It takes more patience and time to assist them." My back was straight and I noticed that I was sitting on the edge of my seat. I tried to relax a little, to appear more confident. I wanted this job so much. It would fix everything. I smiled softly, noticing my accent seemed fuddled. I didn't sound like a New Yorker anymore, but I didn't sound Texan either.

Gus nodded, "Hmm. Interesting observation." I looked at him, slightly intimidated. The man was in his early thirties, blonde hair and blue eyes. He looked like a cover model for GQ, holding my application in his hands. His eyes scanned it again. When he was done, he looked over the top of my papers and pointed his pen at me, "You get points for not giving cookie-cutter answers, Miss Tyndale, but you have no previous sales experience. It says here that you were a minister... in Texas?" The man looked at me like I was insane. As soon as I answered that question, this job interview was over.

Before I could speak a voice came from the shadows at the end of the room. "So, that's where you went? Texas." That voice. It made my stomach flip. My body was instantly covered in goose bumps, every hair standing on end. Something inside my chest ached when he spoke. Although I hadn't heard it in years, I recognized his warm playful tone instantly. I'd know him anywhere.

My pulse quickened and I suddenly felt much more nervous than I had a moment ago. Jaw hanging open, I turned and stared at him like he was a ghost. "Jack?"

CHAPTER FOUR

Leaning against the doorjamb stood Jack Gray, and he was every bit as beautiful as he was the last time I saw him. Dark jeans clung to his trim waist and a black V-neck tee shirt showcased sculpted muscles beneath. His arms were folded over his chest, his head tilted to the side, dark hair spilling into his blue eyes. My pulse ratcheted up a few more notches. I was nervous before, but Jack made me a million times worse. A swarm of butterflies erupted in my stomach, rendering me speechless and stealing my brains. Butterfly bastards.

Jack's soft blue eyes slid over my face, surprised. "Long time, Abby." His lips were set into a thin line, his jaw tight. The tension in his shoulders said he wasn't happy to see me. Pushing himself off the door, he strolled across the room. A pair of Chuck's, covered in paint, adorned on his feet. My heart jumped into my throat. Jack didn't look the way I remembered him, he looked better. It was like my mind had downplayed his looks to trick me into thinking I made him up. Voice still stolen by winged creatures wisping through my insides, I remained silent, with my eyes way too big for my body.

Dark hair hung in his eyes as he looked down at my information. He pointed to something that Gus had written. "This is interesting."

Gus responded, "Would you like to take over, boss?" The way he addressed Jack surprised me. By comparison, it looked like Jack should be Gus' assistant or office boy. He was dressed so casually while Gus was dressed like a businessman, suit and all.

My eyebrows shot up on my face, my hands clutched tightly in my lap, "Boss?" Oh, there's my voice. Think, Abby, think! Jack's the boss. What does that mean for me? The fat walrus in my brain said it meant I was screwed. Damn it!

Gus nodded, glancing up at Jack, then back at me. "Miss Tyndale, this is Jonathan Gray. He's the artist and the owner."

My face felt hot. "Oh, I didn't realize..." Of course not. Why would I realize Jack was the owner? I couldn't fathom why or how that was possible until Gus added, "Jonathan Gray is his penname, a pseudonym. Few people still know him as Jack Gray. As he became more successful his name became problematic—Jack Gray sounds like vodka, not an ambitious painter." Gus crinkled his nose and I was guessing he preferred a bottle of wine to a bottle of Jack. I stared, shocked, as he spoke. If the sign had said Jack Gray, I would have never opened the door. Oh, holy hell. Now what? I wanted the job, but I wanted to get out of there too. My face felt hot. Think Abby, think!

Jack sat down across from me, his perfect body settling into the leather chair, his eyes locking with mine. "What brings you back to New York, Abby?" We'd been friends, once. But I left, and hadn't spoken to him since. Actually, he was part of the reason I ran and didn't look back. Nerves caught up with me and I realized that I was gripping my hands so hard they'd gone numb. Releasing them, I decided to be frank. The job would still fix things, and I still wanted it, even if it meant dealing with Jack.

"I need a job, Jack. Someone told me to try here, so I'm here." It took every ounce of control I had to maintain the lock on his eyes. I wanted to look away. There was something about him—there always was—it was like he could see straight through me.

Jack leaned back in his chair, running his fingers through his dark hair. He let out a breath and sat up straight, pulling my papers in front of him on the table. As he read, he touched his fingers to his lips, "You may have a knack for dealing with people, Abby, but this job requires sales skills that you don't have." Still watching me, he said, "I'll give you the job right now, if you can tell me how to sell a patron a 2.3 million dollar painting. It's the least expensive in my collection."

Someone must have sucked all the air out of the room, because I couldn't breathe, "Million?" I knew I shouldn't have asked, but I had to. This was Jack, for godsakes! The boy that dabbled in paint. But he was more now. A famous artist I didn't know. And the reason that I didn't know was because I didn't talk to anyone we went to school with. I didn't go to our high school reunions. I didn't do Facebook or

Twitter. I'd fallen off the grid, partly to get away from this boy who was now a successful man.

Jack nodded, and steepled his fingers. Head tilted, he said, "I'm serious. How would you sell it, Ab?"

Gus watched the exchange, smart enough not to interfere. The room was charged with emotion from the moment Jack entered. I had no idea what Jack was thinking. His posture said he didn't care, not anymore, but his eyes said something entirely different. That blue gaze was dark, the tiny specs of light extinguished by God-knew-what. Gus leaned back in his chair, his pointer fingers resting against his chin. He tapped it periodically as his eyes shifted between us.

I stared at Jack for a moment, waiting for an answer to come to me, but it didn't. I didn't know how to do sales. Thoughts spilled into my head, things I could have tried to make into a reasonable attempt to sound like I knew what I was talking about, but I didn't know. My stomach sank. Whatever was between us at one point was now one-sided because Jack sat there cooly gazing at me. Once upon a time, he would have realized how much I was squirming inside and put me out of my misery. But not now. Twisting my hands, I confessed, "I'm not sure." My voice was quiet as I looked past Jack to the sea. The steady sound of waves crashing on the beach was nostalgic.

Jack saw my eyes look past him at the water on the other side of the window. He knew how much I loved the beach. "When was the last time you were home?" he asked.

My gaze drifted back to his face, avoiding his eyes. Pushing a stray hair out of my face, I said, "Haven't been. I left and didn't plan on coming back. But things changed, and, well, I got here last night. Today I'm sitting in front of you asking for a job that I need, and want, but can't possibly get." What was I saying? I cringed inside. There was this bravado in my voice mixed with something else I couldn't identify. I had blurted out what I honestly thought with no expectations from Jack.

His voice was deep, surprised, "A job you *want*? You really want to do sales?" Risking another glance at his deep blue eyes I noticed the trail of dark stubble on his cheeks. He was beautiful. My stomach twisted as he looked at me. I nodded. I wanted this job. It would fix everything. The expression on Jack's face led me to believe he might give it to me, but I was wrong. Looking away, he said, "The right answer is that you sell an expensive painting the same way you would sell any other work..." His hands rubbed his face, "How can I give you this position when there are others that are way more qualified? I'm sorry Abby, but this won't work out."

My teeth had taken hold of my bottom lip. I should have known as much. Begging Jack for a job was bad enough. He had a way of making me melt and do stupid things that I wouldn't have normally done. That was the way he was back then—and it only seemed to have intensified with age.

Humiliated, I stood, "Thank you for your consideration. I'll show myself out." As I swung my purse over my shoulder, I walked to the door. I was so screwed. My mind warped into hyper-drive as panic shot through my brain yipping like a freaked-out Chihuahua. I was going to die, eaten by the walrus. The noise of a chair moving behind me caught my ear, but I figured it was just Jack leaving. I didn't expect him to lunge in front of me, stopping me in my tracks.

"Where are you going?" he laughed, throwing his body in front of me so I couldn't walk through the door. His silky dark hair fell in his eyes. The smile melted that cold expression he was giving me before. My heart lurched at the sight of it. It took me a minute to realize he wanted me to stop. I'm kind of thick sometimes. Hands up in the universal sign for stop went right over my head, so he threw himself in front of me. "Abby, I said you couldn't have that job. You'd suck at it." I frowned without meaning to. He smiled in response, his eyes bright and wistful, "I have something better, and it suits you perfectly. Follow me."

Taken aback, I blinked. What did he say? He had another job? Turning, I quickly followed him from the room. Mind reeling, I wondered what job he thought I could do, and wondered exactly how irritated he was with me. Irritated wasn't the right word, but I half expected him to hand me a toilet brush. It wasn't until Gus yelled after him that I thought he might have another real job.

Gus called out, running his fingers through his perfect hair, "Jack, we need to discuss this."

"Later, Gus. It's my call this time. You picked the last one!" Before Jack finished talking he was out the door. I practically ran to keep up. We walked around the exterior of the building. The wind blew gently, taking my long hair and whipping it into my eyes.

CHAPTER FIVE

Jack turned back to me, "That's the main building where everyone else works, but over here— this is where the magic happens," he grinned at me. We'd reached a building that was attached on the side, concealed by sand dunes and tall grass. The long sleek lines of the upper section of the building blended into the sister structure next to it. When Jack threw open the doors, I walked through and entered his studio. My lips parted as I stared. It was huge. No, huge was an understatement. The room looked like an airplane hangar, minus the planes. Camera equipment was suspended from the ceiling, canvases bigger than my house lined the walls, and more canvas was on the floor, thickly coated in paint. Next to it was a board with photographs of a woman pinned to it. I stared harder, trying to see, but I was too far away.

Jack moved around me, careful not to touch me as he passed, asking, "Do you know what I'm famous for, Abby? Do you know why people pay millions for my work?" I shook my head. There were no finished pieces in sight, and I hadn't seen any on the way in. Jack beamed, his beauty amplified in this setting. He explained, "It's part innovation and part seduction. People crave something that is sensual, that reveals the inner workings of the human mind, and I give them that." He grinned, "And the rest was luck. I was in the right place at the right time."

Looking around I said, "I don't understand. Are these the finished paintings?" Maybe he was a minimalist selling blank canvases on stretchers with pretty frames.

"No," he breathed, staring at me, watching my reaction carefully. I stood in front of a large bay of windows; the light spilling through behind me. His eyes lingered a beat too long before moving to a curtain that spanned across the back wall. "This is one of my finished works." Clasping the curtain in his hand, Jack slid it back. As he revealed more and more of the painting, I found myself walking toward it, eyes growing steadily wider, lips parting further and further.

It was evocative and alluring, sensual. It was a myriad of contradictions and promises—a moving story told in paint. There was an abstract quality to the work, but not so much that I couldn't tell what it was. The painting was of a woman, her form captured in wide brush strokes of soft color. The curve of her figure, the expression on her face, and the long hair that drifted down her back made me stare at it. Sensual was the tame word to describe what he painted. It was raw emotion and full ecstasy, captured on canvas.

I couldn't breathe. My face felt hot. I was certain my cheeks were burning. "Jack, this is..." I searched for the right word, but couldn't find one. Stepping closer, I shook my head whispering, "carnal, raw, evocative, and... sexy as hell." My eyes were locked on the painting, on this vision of beauty that he created. When did Jack learn to do this?

His hands were behind his back. Jack was smiling, watching me, standing next to me. "Cursing preacher?"

I shrugged, not looking away from the painting, "I never really had a tame tongue."

"I remember," he said softly. "That mouth of yours used to get you in trouble. Frequently."

My eyes were wide when I turned and looked at him. The expression on his face only deepened my blush. He was genuinely amused, watching my eyes devour his painting like I couldn't get enough. "Preacher girl, I think you like naughty art," he laughed, a dimple showing as his smiled deepened.

Trying to defend myself, I said, "It's not naughty. It's..." but he didn't let me finish.

"Then why are you beat-red?" He laughed, "It's kind of cute. I haven't had this much fun showing my work to anyone in a while. And I never thought I'd be showing it to a nun, and hear her say it's not dirty."

The corners of my mouth twisted up into a smile as I turned my blushing face in his direction, "It's not dirty!" I protested. "It's beautiful. Shockingly sensual. I just didn't think you could paint something like that."

"Why's that?" he asked, the smile fading from his lips.

I shrugged, "I don't know. I just... I've never seen anything like it before. There's so much here. It has the timeless quality of an Old Master's painting, but it has some of the qualities of Pollack's work. It's beautiful." His lips were parted, watching me as I spoke; taking in my every word like it was air. Jack and I were a thing that never happened. We went through high school and he was one of my best friends, but there was more between us. Shaking the thoughts from my mind, I asked, "How did you make this?"

He arched an eyebrow at me, and turned away. "It's um, not what you'd expect."

I laughed, "What do you mean? You didn't use a paint brush?" I was joking, but he shook his head.

"No, it's not like that," he stated, running his hand through his hair. Not looking at me, he stepped toward the painting, looking at it, recounting how it was made. "It's more... unconventional, which is why I always have a female assistant at my studio. It maintains propriety, and that's the difference between my art selling for millions and nothing." Jack was staring at the painting, his jaw tightening like something was bothering him.

"What do you mean?" I asked, turning to look at him. His hands were shoved into his pockets, as he gazed at his sneakers briefly, looking at me from under his brow. He still looked like the boy I knew, not the millionaire man that he was supposed to be. Oddly, Jack seemed to hide his wealth. Getting closer to him, I could see he was wearing the same brands he used to wear. Nothing appeared to change.

His blue gaze pierced mine, "Reputation is the only thing keeping these paintings from being considered porn. Everything rides on my reputation. I don't touch my models, I don't screw the models, and I don't use the same model more than once. And there's always a schoolmarm type sitting here during the shoots. Those things protect my reputation, and keep these as art—sensual representations of the human form." Jack walked next to the painting on the board, and picked up a pile of pictures. They must have been shot with his camera. I didn't really get what he was saying until I looked at them.

Keeping my face still, I flipped through the pile. From one picture to the next, my heart raced harder. When I got to the end of the stack, I looked up at him, eyes wide, "You weren't kidding. You don't use a paint brush."

He shook his head, taking the stack of pictures back. His fingers brushing mine without meaning to. A jolt passed between us. It was like it was before, years ago. I gasped, trying to ignore it. Jack did the same, "The models are the paint brush." He pressed his lips together, glancing at me, as if my approval mattered. "Fine art has always had nudes at the center, and this, this is a similar take on that."

My arms folded across my chest, trying to ease the swirling sensation in my stomach. I wasn't sure if this was scary or fascinating. Probably a little of both. Glancing at him, I asked, "You paint them? And then what?"

Nodding, he walked down the length of the painting, his hands in his pockets. "I paint the model's body, using the color palate I need, and then I instruct her, and tell her what to do." He turned back to me, leaving some space between us, "It's kind of like a life-size stamp. She lies down on the canvas and moves across it as directed. I shoot while the painting is being made," he pointed to the large camera fixed to the ceiling, "and then go back and hand-paint the rest. And this is the end result." He gestured to the finished painting next to him.

Heart racing, I pressed my lips together and asked, "What is it that you want me to do?"

His gaze locked with mine. My stomach stirred. His voice was cool, confident, "I want you to be the marm. No one will question anything with preacher-girl here. Especially if you think these are Kosher." His eyes were twin lakes of endless blue. The spinning sensation abruptly stopped when he said marm. So that's how he saw me.

I swallowed hard. I wanted the job, hell I needed the job, but I didn't think I could take being around him every day. Before I realized what I was saying, I heard my voice speaking, "I don't know."

"Why not?" he asked. "It'd be perfect." Jack pulled his hands from his pockets, drawing my eye to the spot where his dark jeans hugged his narrow hips. The tee shirt he wore made his eyes seem deeper, darker than possible. The soft smile on his lips was electric.

Crushing the feelings he was arousing, I turned away, staring at the art on the wall. I couldn't believe that he still had this effect on me. It was the same way it was the last time I saw him. That moment came rushing back. It was summer, about ten years ago. We stood on the beach, the waves crashing onto the sand behind us. Jack had a horrible reputation during high school. If a girl looked his way, he had to have her. And he did. That didn't jive with my idealistic tendencies. I wanted a soulmate, someone who only felt whole when he was with me. Jack wasn't that person. I'd never met my soulmate, and still haven't. But that night, I felt different. Something happened. We were inches apart and I felt my lips drifting toward his. My hands were tangled in his hair, his hands at his sides. Our eyes were locked, saying everything in silence. As our lips were about to meet, I stopped. Jack hadn't moved, and I didn't want to kiss him if he didn't want it. A kiss meant something to me, and he knew it. I'd told him over and over again how a kiss should mean something, that sex wasn't a sport. It was more than that.

The kiss never happened. I remained still, feeling his breath drift softly across my lips and his silky hair in my hands. He was a breath away, so close. His eyes were lowered, like mine, watching my lips the entire time. My fingers slid down the side of his face, slowly. When my hands reached his chin, I released him. The moment shattered. The kiss was lost, never to be given, never to be taken.

That was so long ago. Why was it bothering me now? Shoving the memory aside, I said, "I just... I need to think about it."

He stepped in front of me, blocking my view of the painting, looking down into my face, "What's there to think about? It pays better than the other job, and you'd have less people to deal with. Just me and the model." He pressed his lips together, "Is it because it's too much? Does the idea of being around nude models bother you?" A normal person would have nodded and said *yes, naked people make me uncomfortable*, and then continued to point out that no one sits next to the naked guy on subway. For some reason, I didn't say that. I felt compelled to tell him the truth. Stupid Abby.

Glancing up at him, I found myself answering before I intended to, "No. I've never had issues with that about art. The human form is one of the most beautiful things in creation." I was a total freak. In Texas, I kept my opinions on art to myself, because they didn't really jive with the culture. They thought nudity was scandalous, as if bare skin was inherently evil and needed to be instantly covered in denim, gingham, and large bows. I thought Jack's painting was interesting—a moment in time, captured in paint, showcasing what people perceived as beauty. Clothing would have ruined it.

"Then what is it?" Jack asked, deadly serious, voice hushed. Before I could answer, he added, "I swear to God, when I heard your voice coming from that room, I couldn't believe it. The hairs on the back of my neck stood up before I even saw you. And then, when I opened the door, and saw you sitting there with Gus... it was like seeing a ghost." There was an expression in his eyes that made me melt.

"I feel like a ghost, Jack." It was strange we were using the same word. It felt like my life was stamped out and I was the walking dead. At the same time, seeing him again, it was too much. Everything was rushing back. Just standing here with him had me in overdrive, trying to fend off that look. Taking this job would save me from one thing and screw me with another. I looked away from him, toward the door, my stomach twisting over and over again. Crap. I couldn't do this. "Thanks for the offer, but I think that I'll have to find something else." I couldn't be in the same room with him. It wasn't the idea of him painting these sensual images, or the naked models, or any of that... it was him.

It was Jack.

"If that's what you want, Abby... but would you do me one favor before you totally turn it down?" his voice was soft.

I glanced up at him, my hand on the knob, ready to run, ready to walk away from Jack and never look back. But that tone, that soft questioning sound of his voice stopped me. It sent currents straight to my heart, melting me, making me want to give him anything he wanted. Turning I said, "Sure. What is it?"

"Come to the session later tonight and see what it is that you'd do. Talk to the woman you're replacing. I think you'd really like it. It's a good job. We start at 8pm. See you then?" Jack's demeanor changed from boyishly shy to bold.

Maybe being around Jack wouldn't be so bad? If he was working, he wouldn't have time to run his sapphire blue eyes over my body and make my heart pound in my chest. He couldn't make me question every decision I've ever made. Going against my better judgment, I said, "Okay. I'll try it."

CHAPTER SIX

I drove back to Kate's thinking I was insane, and she told me as much as soon as she got home from work. Kicking off a pair of commuter shoes, she said, "What the hell are you thinking? You can't take a job like that. Your church won't take you back after that. The whole thing sounds indecent. And I'm a New Yorker! Those Texan crack-pots think dancing is evil, Abby. You live in that little Footloose town, for christsakes! Use your brain! Naked women rolling in paint is way worse than dancing!"

I rolled my eyes, cringing as she said it. No doubt she was right. Back in Texas, anything even remotely sensual was evil. That explained all the clothing starched into sandpaper. Nobody wanted to touch that. But what she said was the perception that Jack tried so hard to diffuse, and I wasn't going to back down. There was nothing wrong with his art. "You don't get it Kate. It's not like that. The paintings were so raw that it was shocking. It showcased beauty, not lust."

Rolling her eyes, she said, "You're a girl, Abby. Guys look at naked chicks and lust. Believe me. You're in uncharted waters here—unless you did it with some random guy and forgot to tell me." Kate walked into the kitchen while we were talking, shirking off her jacket and draping it over the counter.

I blanched at her reference. It was something I didn't talk about with anyone. I was a 28-year-old virgin, by choice. My vows forced me to a life of celibacy, but that didn't mean I was an idiot. Following her, I said, "I don't have to screw someone to see the difference between art and porn, Kate. If you'd seen his work..." I didn't get to finish. She rounded on me, cutting me off.

"I have seen his work! What the hell do you think I do all day? Jonathan Gray is the next big thing. We've been trying to get him to do a show for the past four years! I've seen his work. I know he's good. And I know he'll get your ass canned if you take that job." Kate's steam seemed to ebb a little, and she added, "Abby, it'll end your career. A forced sabbatical was bad enough, but this... There'll be no going back."

I wanted to tell her that she was wrong, but she wasn't. It didn't matter what was right or wrong, or what I believed. This was the catch-22 of being me— sometimes self-preservation kept me from doing what was right. I had to choose my battles, or I'd get strung up by the conservative types that sat in my pews and not get a chance to help anyone. They would say the same things Kate was saying, or worse. If you thought the minister led the church, you thought wrong. It was more like giving a kid a stick and telling him to corral a hundred big, smelly sheep without anything else. You had to be careful who you poked, and sheep weren't the brightest bulbs in the box. It honestly took a lot of restraint to not beat them over the head with the stick. But that was my life. It required unending patience, which I felt was worth it if I saved one person along the way.

Leaning hard on the counter, I hung my head. "Fine. You're right, Kate. You're right." I looked up at her, "I'll have to find something else." I pushed back, and walked into the living room, slumping down onto the couch. It smelled like Kate's perfume. Foiled again by close-minded crazies who weren't even here.

Kate thought I was sulking because of her terse words. "I didn't mean to yell, Abby. I just know how serious this is," she emerged from the kitchen, thigh-highs in one hand and a beer in the other. She tossed the stockings on the table and sat down on her favorite chair, opening the can at the same time. "Those loans are gonna kill you. That church has you trapped. You have to make nice, go back as soon as they'll have you, and find another congregation. Don't stay there. Dropping you on your head during a freak-out was a shitty thing to do."

I rubbed my face, confessing, "It wasn't a freak out."

"Then what was it?" her voice mystified. "What was so intolerable that got them that pissed off?"

Instead of answering, I stood and opened the front closet. Pulling on my coat, I looked back at her.

"I told Jack that I'd see what the job entailed tonight. He has a model and his assistant there." Kate cocked her head and gave me an are-you-retarded look. "I have to go. He had them all come in so I could meet them. I'll humor him for a little bit and then tell him no. You're right, Kate. I'm trapped. The only way out is to survive the next twelve months and then go crawling back, and see if I can salvage things well enough to get me to the next place."

She downed the beer while we were talking, her jaw tight. "I'd pay those off for you, if I could."

Zipping my coat, I answered, "Thanks, but I wouldn't want you to. It was my mistake. I'm the one who has to pay for it."

I reached for the knob, when she called my name, "Abby?" I paused, looking back at her. "Do you want this job? I mean, is this what you would have chosen if you got a do-over? No loans, no bills. Just Abby. Would you choose this? I'm asking because it seems risqué, even to me. I can't imagine you wanting to have anything to do with it."

I considered her question, my lips parted, ready to answer. When I was younger, I loved art classes. I looked forward to them. It was the highlight of my day. Getting to create something, getting to form something beautiful where there had been nothing was an act reserved for God, a gift he bestowed upon artists. I couldn't paint the way Jack did, but even then I knew I liked being there, near him. Seeing what he created and watching his gift spin things of beauty to life before my eyes. Nodding, I said, "Yeah, I'd want this job."

CHAPTER SEVEN

I arrived at the studio about an hour later. Jack was talking to an older woman dressed in a suit. A model sat on a stool with a robe draped around her; shapely legs were crossed at the ankle. She watched Jack, waiting for him to instruct her.

When Jack looked up as saw me, his face lit up. It made my stomach sink. I planned on telling him that I couldn't take the job right away, but I couldn't.

Taking me by the hand, his touch sizzling on my skin, he led me into the room. Jack didn't seem to realize what he did to me. He presented me to the model and the marm. Both were courteous.

Jack seemed excited. He walked me over to the older woman. Pale blonde hair was done stylish and short, framing her round face. Glittering brown eyes looked up at me. She sat aside from Jack and the model, a table to her left where she had a cup of coffee. Jack told her, "Abby's an old friend. Tell her exactly what you think about anything she asks, Emily. Okay?"

Emily smiled at me, taking my hand and leaning in close, "An old friend! Well, that will work out wonderfully for Jack. This position is important, but it also needs to be someone he trusts immensely. His career depends on your word. A few vicious words would destroy him."

I nodded, curious. I could see what Kate meant, that this job sounded like debauchery at its finest. Settling next to Emily, I asked "How long have you been working here?"

"About three years. I took this job after I retired for something to do. Seeing Jack work is a real treat. When inspiration sparkles in his eyes, I can't help but get excited with him. People like that are rare, you know." The older woman had fine lines on her face that I hadn't seen before.

"Yes, they are," I looked back at Jack. The model had disrobed and was sitting in the buff on a stool. Her curves were perfect, her skin was smooth, and her hair hung in long curls that had been clipped to the back of her head. Jack's brush was gliding over her neck in slow thick strokes, his eyes focused. "May I ask why you're leaving?" I tore my gaze away from Jack and the model. I felt like a voyeur, even though they weren't doing anything bad.

"The husband wants to escape the rough winters and go further south, so we're moving. I heard you were from the south, is that right?" she asked kindly, her hands folded properly in her lap. I nodded. Emily gazed at Jack and the model. "It's important to keep him in your line of sight at all times. The model can move around, but it's Jack you want to follow." Emily's dark eyes remained on Jack as he smoothed the brush over the girl's skin.

"Why's that," I asked, turning to Jack, my throat growing tighter.

"Well, most people will tell you to watch for the offender. In this case, the model is the one that would cause the problem. If she decides to sell her story of the time Jonathan Gray molested her, everyone will ask what Jack did, where he was, what he said. He's more important than the girl. Always follow his movements. And if he needs you, you're the one that touches the model."

I nearly choked. Jerking my head toward her, I asked, "What? Why would he need that?"

She laughed at me, "You're a bigger prude than me!" Jack turned to look at us, and I blushed. Great. Emily began speaking again and Jack turned his back on us, allowing us to continue our conversation. "You're a sweet girl. A girl who can blush is a girl who can protect Jack. Now, see how he's painting that girl?" I nodded. Jack's brush was working its way down her onto her chest. He dipped the brush in more paint and smoothed a line down her breast. His eyes were narrow, fixated as if he was focusing intensely. It wasn't the gaze of a man in the throes of passion. Not that I'd seen that too often. Or at all. "When he needs to paint her hair, you'll need to help. Otherwise, paint will bleed together and ruin his creation."

Turning, I looked back at Jack. One breast was covered and he was working on the second. Long lines of pale colors covered the girl's body. Jack worked quickly. "So, he paints the girl's body, then her face? Then her hair?"

Emily nodded, "Usually…. unless he's doing a piece limited to the face, which is rare these days. Most of his works have the woman's curves through the hips. Every inch of the model gets painted with organic paint. It doesn't stain her skin and it won't make her hair disgusting. It washes out with that solvent over there." She pointed to a large jug near all the cans of paint spread out around Jack. "It's mostly hand soap, but Jack said there is something else in it, too. The shower is in the back. You stay with Jack when she cleans up. Never leave him alone." I watched Jack as she spoke. The way he held the brush, the curve of his strong arms made it hard for me to look away. He pushed his hair out of his face, accidentally running paint through it.

"How long does this take," I asked, and then flushed when Jack's brush painted over the model's nipple, and dropped below her breasts.

Emily wasn't watching me. Her gaze stayed on Jack. "About twenty minutes for the paint application, depending on what he does with the hair. Then he does the initial stamp, and shoots her with the camera. Total time is usually an hour or two."

"Wow, that's it?" Emily glanced at me out of the corner of her eyes.

"Yup. Pays good for a couple of hours a night. Jack usually works in spurts too. He'll take in several models over a few weeks, painting nearly every night. Then he only uses the one from that lot that he likes the most. The rest get tossed." Her gaze was back on Jack, her eyes tracing the movement of his arm. "Never comment to reporters. Always make sure the shades are dropped when he's painting. And make sure you remain beyond reproach." She smiled, "Shouldn't be hard for a preacher, since that's part of that job, too. So," she changed the direction of the conversation, "Your congregation doesn't have a problem with this?"

"They haven't said so," I replied. It was a lie, but it didn't have the acidic taste I expected. I was mad at them. And there was no way I was telling them that I was doing this. They said survive. This was surviving. Emily didn't press the matter. She stopped talking and we both watched Jack cover the naked woman in paint, until he called me over. My heartbeat doubled, blood rushing through me like a rocket. I shouldn't be doing this.

Jack's blue eyes were on me, grinning. "I need to paint her hair, but we have to make sure it doesn't touch her skin." The model was covered in paint, front and back. The only part that Jack hadn't painted was her eyes.

"What do you need me to do?" I asked, unsure if I was going to do it or not.

Jack shook his head, trying to get a wisp of hair out of his face. "Unclip her hair and after I apply the paint, hold it away from her body. No drips. This is the last step before applying her to the canvas." A large roll of canvas was laid out on the floor. It was bigger than my bed, but smaller than the massive painting behind the curtain. "Don't worry," he added glancing at me, "I'll tell you what to do so it doesn't get messed up." His words lured me to him. Apparently I was doing this.

Taking several containers of pale paint, Jack cracked open the lids while I unclipped the model's hair. She sat perfectly still. I wondered what was going through her head. Jack told her to lean back. The girl arched her back, her hair reaching toward the floor, nearly falling out of my hands. The position left the model holding onto the chair with her breasts in the air, her head tipped back as far as it would go. Jack ignored the seductive pose, but I froze. This was much more than I thought. For some reason it didn't register until I was standing next to Jack.

He grinned, as he lifted a strand of curled hair and dipped it in the paint. "Why, Miss Tyndale, you seem to be blushing again," he teased.

"I didn't realize I would be this close to the model," I said softly, feeling odd that the girl could hear me. Jack dipped another piece of hair, and I took it from him, holding it away from the girl's naked body. Awkwardness consumed me. This was beyond weird. Seeing other girls naked in the locker room was one thing, seeing a nude woman in a painting was another—and this by comparison, well there was no comparison. It was just really strange.

"I don't bite," the girl said, trying not to smile and ruin her paint. Jack grinned.

"That's not what I meant, but thank you for not biting me," I replied, feeling like a dork.

Jack laughed, shaking his head. Continuing, he dipped each tendril in paint until her whole head was dripping. It took about five more minutes and he was done. The girl was a monochromatic rainbow of white. "Okay, this is the tricky part," Jack said. "We need to help her move from the stool, to the canvas. She only has one chance to lay on this correctly. If she messes it up, we start over. If we drop her, we start over. Got it?"

"If we drop her?" I squealed. "Jack, what the hell? You said no touching!"

The model laughed, glancing at Jack, "Your nun cursed!"

"I think she's allowed to say Hell, Cheri. It's a noun and it's in the Bible," the corners of his mouth lifted, laughingly.

"Shut up," I laughed back, shaking my head. I'd been around New Yorkers for less than two days and my mouth was already regressing to its former sailor-like state. "How do I help her?"

"Her right hand has no paint. If she were a lefty, it'd be her left. She's going to put her other hand on the canvas as you lower her holding the paint-free hand. It'll keep her from slipping or hitting the canvas too hard."

Emily spoke up from her seat by the table, "Do you want help, Jack?"

Without looking at her, Jack answered, "Sure, but you stay there. You can tell Abby if you see her doing something wrong," Jack answered.

While they spoke my mind replayed, *I can't believe I'm doing this* over and over. There was nothing wrong with helping a naked woman covered in paint lay down on a canvas, but it felt really weird. I held up her hair with one hand and took her dry hand with my other. "What about her hair? I won't be able to hold her hand and her hair once she leans back onto the canvas."

"You don't have to," Emily said. "Once her hair is over the canvas, let go. It'll fall where it's supposed to go. Basically, you're making a snow angel here, Abby. You'll get a crappy one if she hits the canvas wrong." I nodded.

Jack looked at me, a small grin on his lips. "Ready?" The model was positioned at the edge of the canvas, her bare feet next to it. Cheri nodded and took my hand in hers. Jack began to tell Cheri what he wanted her to do. "Go down on your side. I want your face to press into the canvas, and then roll back. Make sure your arm is at shoulder height, so there is a clear impression of the side of your breast. Abby will fan your hair and then we'll do the rest."

Swallowing hard, I did as he asked, and lowered the girl without dropping her. Cheri's hand was about shoulder height when I finished lowering her to the floor. Her skin slid over the canvas like the paint was still totally wet.

"How long does it take for the paint to dry?" I thought it should have been tacky by now.

Jack watched Cheri closely as he answered, "A few hours. There's something in it to keep it from drying too fast." He said to Cheri, "Good. That's perfect. Now roll back and Abby will fan your hair." He looked up at me when Cheri stopped moving. This was weird. There was a naked girl at my feet, but he didn't look at her the way he was looking at me. "Take off your shoes so you don't get dirt onto the canvas." I did as he said and padded past the naked woman, to her head.

Jack gave more directions, "Take each strand of hair and fan it that way, like the wind is blowing." I nodded and moved the pieces were he told me to put them. "That looks perfect. Okay, before you come back, press her hair down with your hands to make sure it left the impression. Be careful not to leave handprints." Her hair was filled with paint, each twisting curl left a multi-tonal impression on the canvas.

The rest of the shoot went well. Jack shot a few pictures before the model moved. He told her what to do and exactly how to position her body. The paint smeared under her, leaving impressions of her curves as she went. I stood next to Emily, watching Jack for the next hour. He knew exactly what he wanted, and didn't stop until he got it. When Jack was done, Emily reached for Cheri and hoisted her up.

Cheri looked down at her body, smeared with paint. Then she said, "Good night, Jack. Good luck." She smiled warmly at all of us before leaving through a side door. The water turned on in the back when Cheri jumped in the shower to wash off.

Emily nodded to Jack, picking up a granny sweater and wrapping it around her shoulders. "It was wonderful to meet you, Abby. Best of luck, Jack." She smiled at him, before leaving the studio.

Jack wiped his hands on a towel, before tossing it to me. "So, what'd you think?"

I caught the towel and wiped the paint off my hands. "It made me blush more than I thought it would."

"Everything makes you blush, Tyndale," he smiled, "but do you think it's something you could do?" He leaned back against the stool, flexing his arms. The curves of his chest pressed tightly against his tee shirt.

My throat felt tight. "Maybe, but..."

"But what?" Jack's expression shifted from playful to careful. "Abby, it's clean. You saw me. When I'm painting, it's not a naked woman. Everything is shadow and light. Lines and curves. Tell me you saw that on my face. You had to see it."

"I did," I answered looking down, my hair spilling over my shoulders. "I'm not sure what was going through your mind, but it probably wasn't the look of a man filled with lust." He was a few steps away from me, watching me while I spoke.

Pushing off the stool, he stepped toward me, folding his arms over his chest, "Probably?" he asked, tilting his head. I bit my bottom lip. I didn't mean to tell him that. Kate knew that I was a virgin because she guessed. I blushed, feeling his gaze on my face. Jack inched closer, "Preacher girl, have you been alone all these years?"

Cheri chose that moment to throw open the changing room door. Jack stepped back, looking at me oddly. Cheri smiled, fully clothed, wet hair drawn back by a headband. "You did great Abby. Really. I've worked with several painters and I was dying to work with Jack. When Emily told me she wouldn't be assisting, I was a little worried, but you did great." She pressed her hands together, and turned to Jack, "I hope you pick mine, Jack! You'll let me know, right?"

Jack nodded, his eyes drifting off my face slowly, like he didn't want to. Turning toward Cheri he said, "Yeah, the office will tell you if it gets hung in the gallery. Be sure to pick up your check from Linda on the way out, and there's a referral slip there for you, too."

The girl beamed. "You have no idea how badly I wanted that referral! Thank you, Mr. Gray!" she went to hug him, and stopped herself, "Sorry! I forgot. Have a good night!" She beamed and practically ran through the door.

Surprised, I looked at Jack. "Referral slip?"

He nodded, wandering through the room, shutting off the lights. "Yeah, it makes it easier for them to get better gigs if they have a slip from me. As long as they don't fall or creep me out, I give them one. Good job not dropping her. She would have been pissed," a grin lit up his face as he turned.

"Jack, wait." I followed him to the back of the room. He was rimmed in light as he turned his head toward me. "I can't do this. I can't take this job. I won't be able to go back to work when I'm done if I take it. It'll kill my career." Actually, I wasn't sure if I cared if it killed my career, but those loans weren't going away, and the only way to get rid of them was to remain in my current profession.

Jack looked down at the tiled floor in the changing room. Dark hair obscured his face so I couldn't quite see him. His voice was soft, "You're not here for good?"

"I hope not," I answered a little too eagerly, hastily adding, "I'm on sabbatical."

He nodded, pressing his lips together tightly before looking up at me. "You think that they wouldn't have you back after working for me? Like this? That it's wrong?" His eyes bore into me, searching for an answer. What people thought of him seemed to matter more than I had thought it did.

I stepped toward him, keeping my eyes on his. My voice soft, "It's not wrong, Jack. It's art. And art's subjective. But, I live in the middle of nowhere, in one of the most conservative states in the country. I have to pay attention to what people think."

His voice was cold, "Okay." Turning, Jack flipped off the light. The room was pitch-black. He flicked the switch and the blinds pulled up, letting moon light spill into the room, before moving toward the door to leave.

"Don't sound like that. Jack, wait." His back was turned toward me; he was walking away. I don't know why I did it. I didn't mean to. I reached out for his shoulder. When my fingers rested there, he froze. Shoulders tense, he turned, looking down at me.

"What's right, Abby? It's not a hard question. Either condemn me or condone me, but don't sit on the fence and pretend to be something you're not."

His words were sharp, the muscle in his jaw tightening.

I shook my head, "You don't understand."

His voice remained frigid. "No, Abby, I do. I really do." Jack turned and started to walk. My brain played flashbacks, assaulting me with memories that plagued my dreams, turning them into nightmares. And I didn't think he was wrong. There was nothing bad about this. In moments of panic people do stupid things. They have a split second to make a decision and you can tell exactly how crazy they really were, and I was bat-shit crazy. I solved one problem and flirted with a million more.

I blurted it out before I could stop myself, "I'm not on the fence, Jack. Your work is divine. I've never seen it's equal. Ever. I'm on your side. I'll do it!" And you can't stop me! Ha! I was breathing hard, my face flushed with excitement. Jack stopped walking. Slowly, he turned back to look at me. I continued, feeling my pulse rising as he looked at me like my words had an effect on him. "You're right. If it's not wrong, then I have nothing to hide and neither do you."

Moving back to me, he looked down, "You really think that?" His voice was deep, and the way he looked at me made my stomach clench. Parts of me that I hadn't felt in years were suddenly on fire. The way his eyes lingered on mine, the set of his jaw and slant of his shoulders, it felt like I was melting under his gaze. Jack was caught between disbelief and awe.

Nodding slowly, I looked away from him. I couldn't say it to his face, "You've always been an amazing artist Jack, but this—what you do here—it's jaw-dropping for so many reasons. You appreciate beauty, but it's so much more than that. Each painting is like a living thing. I've never seen that before. You've taken all the best attributes of the art world and compiled them into one thing, one beautifully stunning thing. It took my breath away when you pulled back the curtain earlier." My voice grew softer as I spoke.

I could feel Jack's eyes on the side of my face as I tried to look anywhere but at him. When I stopped speaking, the room was utterly silent. The only sound remaining was the muffled noise of the waves crashing onto the sand. When I turned back to look at Jack, I couldn't tell what he thought. His head was tilted to the side, his arms folded like he was mad, but his eyes said something else. I just didn't know what. "It's late. I better go. Kate will wonder what happened to me."

Jack nodded, silently walking me to my car. Before I reached for the door, he held out his hand. When I looked down I saw a slim, sleek, iPhone. "Take it. I need to be able to get in touch with you in case the shoot times shift. Sometimes there's drama with the models." He shrugged like it was nothing.

I stared at his hand, shaking my head, "I can't take that." Cell phones were expensive, and I couldn't afford to pay the bill. Before I could protest more, Jack grabbed me by a belt loop with one hand and shoved the phone into my pocket with the other. I gasped, my jaw hanging wide open.

Jack laughed when he saw the look on my face, "It's a job requirement, Abby, and I know you don't have a cell. Take it. You need it. It's a company phone, so it's not like you get to keep it forever. We're only footing the bill while you work here." He pointed at the phone as I pulled it out of my pocket. "My number is programmed into the thing. If you're late, call." I slid into the car, knowing I'd have to take it. "Same time tomorrow. See you then." Jack was distant again, all the warmth and playfulness from earlier was gone. I felt like I was going to hurl. I'd said too much. I nodded and drove off with a sinking feeling in my stomach.

CHAPTER EIGHT

"You did not! Abby, what they hell are you thinking?" Kate scolded. First she was mad because it was nearly 2:00am and she thought someone killed me and buried me on the beach. Second, she was pissed because she thought I'd made a really stupid decision. Third, she went nuclear when she realized Jonathan Gray was Jack Gray. I shouldn't have told her that. Ooops.

Irritated, I grabbed a glass from the cabinet and walked to the sink, flicking on the faucet. "I already told you. There's nothing wrong with it. There's no lust/ porn element, and having me there will make sure it stays that way."

Her dark hair fell over her shoulders as she leaned over the counter, "Abby, he'll drag you down with him. What if the press sees you? What if there's a scandal in the next year? Do you really want to risk it all for this? For him?" I looked away from her, chugging my water like it was air. I didn't want to justify myself to her, but in the back of my mind—I knew that if I couldn't make Kate see that it was all right, there was no way the church board would be okay with it. Before berating me more, she leaned back. Her jaw dropped open, "Oh my God. It's him, isn't it?"

Startled, I turned to look at her. "What are you talking about?"

"It's Jack Gray. He's turned your head," she smiled mischievously at me. Kate could sniff things out like a bloodhound. I blanched as she teased, half sighing while she smiled, "Abby's got a crush."

I stiffened, placing my glass in the sink. "It's not like that. It can't be like that..."

"Lust doesn't cancel out just because you took a vow, Abby." She grinned like the Cheshire cat, green eyes glinting.

I stiffened, appalled at her suggestion, "It's not lust! Good night!" I walked away from her, slapping my bare feet down the hallway like a petulant child, and slammed my bedroom door.

Behind me, I heard her laughing, "Call it what you want, but you have the hots for Jack Gray!"

CHAPTER NINE

The next morning things seemed better with Kate. She was all chatter and smiles. It was Saturday, so she didn't have to go into the city. Since I had no money, we couldn't go shopping or get a coffee, but I really wanted to be outside, so we went to the village to hang out. The streets were lined with shops of all sorts, and the beach wasn't far away. Kate strolled beside me, nodding at the people she knew every so often as we walked.

"I did some research on Mr. Fabulous. You wanna hear?" she asked suddenly when we stopped in front of the bakery.

My nose was assaulted by the scent of sugar and yeast, and I was in a good mood. "Sure, why not? What'd you find, Kate?"

Before answering, Kate said, "I'm buying you a cookie or something. You're staring through the glass like a homeless chick." She grabbed my hand and pulled me through the door. I was protesting, but I lost my focus when that door opened. The scent alone was enough to make me move back to New York. There weren't places like this where I lived in Texas. My mouth was salivating as we stood in line, staring at a refrigerator case filled with millions of tiny cookies, beautifully decorated pastries, and cakes that put all others to shame.

"Well, Jack sold his first painting about eight years ago. It went on auction at a benefit and sold for over $200,000. That auction is what propelled him into stardom. Suddenly, he was discovered and had patrons breathing down his neck, wanting more art like the one he'd given away. Jack didn't get a dime from that first sale. It all went to charity." We inched up to the glass when the person in front of us left. Kate ordered two giant butter cookies covered in mini chocolate chips. After she paid, we walked back outside and continued strolling toward the docks. "Oh my god, these are good." She bit off another piece of cookie and continued, "After that, he continued to sell racy art to the affluent. He only paints models, which is interesting since he did have some patrons who wanted their portrait made like that. Rumor has it that he turned down a multimillion dollar commission, because the patron insisted on being the model and Jack wouldn't have it."

"Holy shit," I didn't mean to say it, but I couldn't believe my ears. Kate laughed at me, spewing cookie, nearly choking while I asked, "Who was it? Who would offer that much money and insist on being in the painting?"

"Forget that!" she said. "Who would turn down that much money? It makes me wonder, it really does."

I glanced at her, wiping away cookie crumbs that were hugging my lips, "Wonder what?"

We stopped walking. She tilted her head at me, "Wonder what's wrong with him. Guess which painting that would have been if he painted it?" I shook my head. I would have assumed it would have been after he had some money and felt okay turning it down. It had to be after he knew where his next meal was coming from. But Kate shocked me again, "Number two. He was broke, Ab, and turned down all that money on principle."

My jaw dropped, eyes going wide. I swallowed hard, nearly choking on my coveted cookie. I stared at Kate for a moment, too stunned to speak. Last night when I spoke to Jack, I could tell how important it was to him that people knew he was beyond reproach, but turning down millions to paint a patron... that sounded insane. Especially when you know broke the way we knew broke—Ramen noodles, toilet paper doubling as tissues, and should I buy dinner or pay the electric bill kind of broke.

Kate continued, "That's what got him more media attention. The poor kid that turned down nearly three million bucks on principle. The public ate it up, and clients poured out the woodwork. Jack's been able to do things on his terms since then. His principles helped him get to where he is."

Breaking off a piece of cookie, I muttered, "Same here, with less successful results." I sighed. Things worked out for Jack, and I was happy for him. But I wasn't so lucky.

Kate swallowed the rest of her cookie and asked, "You ready to talk about it yet? Or are you just going to continue to make obscure references to what you did down in Texas that pissed off pews filled with crazy, rich white people?"

We walked out onto a pier and sat at the end. "Obscure references for a while longer. Just until I decide if what I did was right or not."

An expression of shock washed across her face, "You don't know? How could you not know if it was right or wrong, Abby?"

I glanced at her, "It was definitely wrong. I just don't know if it was justified, if I should have. They obviously didn't think so." I wanted to come to my own conclusions on this, before I told her. I smiled at her. "I'll tell you soon."

Kate looked out at the deep blue water. It lapped at the wooden pier, and the sky was gray, ready to rain. "There's actually something that I'd like to know more."

"What's that?" I asked, not really paying attention.

"Do you really think you can resist him?" her lips were smashed together. She knew she just asked a loaded question. I must have looked at her with venom, because she held up her hands in surrender, "I come in peace, Ab!" she laughed. "I'm just thinking about you—about the life you chose—does Jack fit into it?"

Swallowing hard, I wanted to answer her, and bite off her head, but Kate was right. I looked down at the water. "As a friend, he fits perfectly."

"And as something more?"

I didn't look up at her, "There can never be anything more. I'd have to turn my back on everything I believe, and I already know Jack's not the guy for me. I didn't tell you this when it happened, but Kate—I almost kissed him once."

Her green eyes were as big as saucers, her jaw hanging open as she stared at me. "When! How could you not tell me?"

I shrugged it off like it was nothing, even though it wasn't. "I didn't tell anyone. It was kind of embarrassing. Before I left, I nearly kissed him. We were so close, but he didn't kiss me, Kate. When I touched his face, he froze, like I disgusted him. It was horrible, like I completely misunderstood him. I'm not making that mistake again, so you don't have to worry about Jack, and neither do I."

CHAPTER TEN

My opinion of Jack was soaring. I couldn't believe what he did—that his success was from doing what he thought was right and helping the poor. It blindsided me, revealing another facet of Jack Gray that I didn't know existed. I couldn't even get my congregation to tithe ten percent, and they still pitched a fit when we didn't spend the tithes on the church building. But Jack, he seemed to have a fundamental sense of right and wrong. When he thought I couldn't see that, he was angry—hurt. But now, after working together for several days, I couldn't see anything else.

I went to the studio, night after night for over a week. Jack was always smiling, excited at the start of every session even though I could tell he hadn't really found the look he was after, not yet. That didn't affect his mood. When Jack was painting, he was in his element and happy. Once he started, his concentration kicked in and he didn't speak until he was giving directions at the end of the session. The process Jack created made the paintings extraordinary, even if he didn't finish most of them. A few lucky paintings would be pulled from the pile and completed. At any given time Jack had about a dozen paintings in his collection. It was this collection that patrons could browse and purchase from. One of the gallery girls said Jack sold them quickly, usually within a year or so. It gave him the means to own this pricy plot of land and pay his employees very well. Jack seemed to donate a lot of his fortune as well. He didn't say anything, but I saw one of the letters on his desk thanking him for his generous contribution with way too many zeros to be real—but it was. And Jack was real, no matter how fairytale-like he seemed.

As I sat and watched him paint model after model, I expected the feeling in the pit of my stomach to subside. There was something about watching the movement of the brush on bare skin, and the look in his eyes when he did it—like nothing else existed—it was alluring. I found that I wanted to watch him paint, that those moments were both awkward and exciting.

The images strewn across the paint took my breath away, not only because of their beauty but because of their raw, evocative nature. In short, the paintings were hot. The way in which he achieved those sensual pieces of art was so far from the dirty things that people thought. Jack's art was hauntingly beautiful. The images were burned into my mind, and seeing how he made them only made it more incredible. His directions were so cold and mechanical, the total opposite of what I'd thought he'd be while creating.

Just as I found my groove and wasn't concerned about dropping the models anymore, I dropped a model. It wasn't really my fault, but it was completely my fault. It was about two weeks after I started, Jack and I were at the studio alone with a model. That part was normal. What wasn't normal was the hollering lunatic that came barging in just when we were stamping the model, Rose, onto the canvas. Rose had her hand stretched out behind her, ready to do what Jack wanted. I held her other hand firmly, and was using my butt as a counterweight. My feet were slipping toward the canvas as I tried to hold her still and lower her at the same time. Jack's eyes flew to the door when he heard the voice outside. His eyes blazed with fury when the woman threw open the studio doors and came traipsing in like she owned the place.

"Jonathan Gray," she snapped her fingers at him, commanding him to come like a dog. Gus appeared behind her with an apologetic look on his face. The witch snapped twice more.

That's when it happened. The model turned her head to see what was going on, and the tiny movement made my already slick hands lose hold of her. The model went crashing down onto the canvas, as I fell backwards onto my butt. All the air was forced out of Rose's lungs as her back hit the hard floor. Knowing Jack couldn't touch the naked, painted, girl, I scrambled over to help her up—my sneakers getting covered in paint.

Jack was furious, "What are you doing here, Belinda? The Galleria is closed and I'm working."

A designer suit clung to her body, revealing every ample curve. Her long hair was elegantly plated into an elaborate hairstyle at the nape of her neck. The dark suit made her sandy hair seem darker. She sneered at him. "Yes, I see." She made a disgusted face at me and Rose on the canvas. "Looks more like porn than art. Two girls wrestling on a slick canvas? Jack…" She tutted him, waving a finger at him like he was a naughty puppy.

Jack practically growled, "Get out before I throw you out." He turned his back on her, ready to storm away, but her words stopped him.

"It's only a matter of time, Jack." The tone of her voice was sharp. Her meaning wasn't clear to me, but it was to Jack. He turned and glared at her. The woman smiled, "When you change your mind, let me know." She pressed a card down on the counter, turned on her heel, and sashayed out with Gus on her heels.

Still helping Rose up, I asked, "Are you okay?"

The girl nodded. Paint dripped from her hair, rolling down her breasts and splattering onto the floor. She rubbed the back of her head where it hit the ground, "I'm fine. She just startled me."

Jack turned back to see both of us covered in paint, standing on the canvas. He closed his eyes, and raked his hands through is hair. "Rose, we're done. Go change. I'll call your manager and reschedule."

The girl looked disappointed, but nodded and headed toward the back of the studio to shower. I watched Jack as he tried to ignore me. The tension that straightened his spine when that woman walked into the room hadn't abated. He was still on edge. Jack moved to his paints, slowly covering them. I walked over and grabbed a lid, hammering it back on. When I reached for another lid, Jack was still kneeling next to me. Reaching out, he covered my hand, stilling me. There was paint everywhere. The model tracked it across the floor, and so had I. Somehow, Jack never had a drop on him, save his sneakers. But, when he placed his hand on top of mine, he brushed his thumb over my hand once, smearing the paint. He sat down hard on the floor after releasing me.

His legs were pulled up to his chest, his arms draped over his knees. Jack's gaze was downcast, "Thanks for helping her. I haven't had a model fall in... well, not since I first started. What a fucking nightmare." He shook his head, and looked up.

Gus came running in spewing apologies, "I'm sorry, Jack. I tried to keep her out, but she wouldn't have it. I haven't seen her this pissed-off since you turned her down."

"What the fuck got her so riled up?" Jack asked, eyes burning with rage as he glanced up at Gus. I swallowed hard. I hadn't heard Jack angry like that, ever. I expected the harshness of his voice and the venom of his words to make me like him less, but it only made me more intrigued.

Gus shrugged, "The hell if I know," then he looked at me, nodded, and added, "Sorry, Abby."

People did that to me all the time. When they did something that they felt was wrong, they looked at me and apologized, like I could put in a pardon for them or something. The truth was that I didn't care that they swore. I still had that wicked tongue inside of me, but I tried to control it. They didn't. Jack stared at me, an unreadable expression on his face. It was in response to Gus' comment. Jack got to his feet and stormed out of the room. I don't know what I did.

Gus still stood in the door way. He walked inside and threw himself into a chair, running his fingers through his light hair. "I didn't think it was possible, but I just pissed him off more. Fuck."

Watching the man, I asked, "What are you talking about?"

Gus sighed, his hands dropping to his sides, "I don't know. I can just tell. I lived with the guy for four years while we were in college. After being around someone that much, you know when you just dumped gasoline on a fire. Believe me. I just made it worse."

The model appeared in the back of the studio, her hair dripping wet. She looked down at the ruined canvas. My sneaker prints were all over it along with a hard mark where her butt hit the canvas before slamming her head into the floor. Rose's expression was cold, and directed at me. "Tell Mr. Gray that he needn't bother rescheduling. I'm not coming back here, not after this." She glared at me. Where did that come from? She didn't think we invited Belinda inside to wreck her session, did she?

Gus jumped to his feet, following the girl as she stormed from the building. Shaking my head, I tried to understand what happened. I got who Belinda was, at least I thought I did. My guess was that she was the shrew who insisted on being the patron covered in paint. No one came back into the studio, so I cleaned up by myself. By the time I'd recovered all the paint cans and cleaned the brushes, it was already past midnight. I grabbed a sponge and started to wipe the foot prints off the floor when Jack came back. I was singing softly to myself, on my hands and knees, scrubbing my sneaker marks away.

When the movement of his shadow caught my eye, I scrambled back and screamed. Jack laughed as I fell on my butt, clutching my heart. "Damn, Jack! Don't sneak up on me like that!" I wasn't sure if I felt most stupid for falling over or for his catching me singing. I threw the damp sponge at his head.

Grinning he caught it between his hands. "Get up, Abby. The cleaning staff does this crap, not you."

"I didn't know what to do. Everyone left, and it was a mess..." I was rambling. He cut me off.

Reaching for my hand, he said, "Come on. Let's get out of here for a while." The rage in his eyes had died down to embers. His hand was extended toward me, waiting for me to grab it.

He's just a friend. Nothing more. I reached out and took his palm. When it slid against mine, my heart lurched. I was such a mess. Was Kate right? Was this incredibly stupid? Jack was a friend—he'd been a good friend until I messed it up.

CHAPTER ELEVEN

Without a word, Jack pulled me outside and down to the beach. We walked along the shore for a while in silence. The moon was huge, even though it was waning. The breeze lifted my hair off my neck. It felt good. It felt good to be home again. It felt good to be near Jack again. The artist stopped walking and sat down, patting the sand next to him for me to follow. We were away from the studio now. The only light that illuminated the sand was from the moon. Lowering myself, I sat next to him and tucked my legs close to my body.

"Abby, I'm sorry about that. That kind of thing doesn't normally happen around here." He shook his head, dark hair falling into his eyes. "That woman has made my life a living Hell."

Carefully, I asked, "Who is she?" I gazed at the waves, watching Jack out of the corner of my eye.

"She was a patron, back before I was successful." Working his jaw, Jack chose his words carefully. "We were a couple for a while, but it didn't work out. She was pissed that I wouldn't paint her, and then doubly pissed when the news hit the papers. It didn't matter that I didn't leak the story, she was still angry." He paused for a moment and glanced at me. The expression on his face made me want to wrap my arms around him and hug him. Knowing that would be stupid, I wrapped my arms around my knees, tightly gripping my legs until my hands turned white.

Jack's expression softened. He looked back at the water as he relived a piece of his past that he clearly wished hadn't happened. "Back then, I did things the way most painters did—the model was the patron. And, well—you know—fine art has nudes. But people said stuff, Abby, and I didn't like what they were saying. She was the first patron I turned down. It turned out that it was better to separate things."

When he didn't continue I asked, "What do you mean?"

"Just that—it's better to keep stuff separate. It seems kind of obvious now. You know, not dating the patrons, not screwing the models—stuff that has the potential to mess with you later—setting up boundaries to keep your personal and professional lives apart." He glanced at me without turning his head. "They failed to teach me that in college. That fucking mistake still haunts me."

Without meaning to, I was staring at him. As he spoke his voice seemed so strained. Turning back to the sea, I said, "Yeah, college kind of sucks like that. They give you book smarts, but completely lack the ability to make you ready for life. That was $300 grand well spent." My tone was sarcastic. School was a sore spot for me. Jack's eyes bulged when I said it, but I continued rambling so he couldn't ask why the hell I took out $300,000 in loans. "You know—I couldn't believe it—when I heard what you did. That's something they couldn't have taught you at college either. It's beyond incredible. You turned down millions. You gave away your first windfall. Who does that?"

"Masochistic people who are content being beggars," he replied, grinning. His eyes were locked on my face as I spoke. There was something about talking about his work that seemed to make him squirm. His voice lightened a little. There was a moment of silence, but I could tell Jack was trying to say something. "Abby...?" I looked directly at him. My breath caught in my throat. His dark hair was tussled by the wind, his eyes endless orbs of blue. "I don't know how to treat you."

Surprised, I asked, "What?" Smiling at him, my stomach fluttered. "What do you mean?"

His hand was in the sand, next to mine. He pressed his fingers into the grains before looking up to me. "We're not the same as we were, but you still feel like the same old Abby. But you're not. You're a nun." I started to protest, but he waved me off, "I know what you're gonna say, but it's so totally the same. It means you're off limits. And what'd I do? I took a nun down to the beach. I have a nun helping me paint nude women. It's weird." My heart sank, and I looked away from him. Before I knew what happened, he gently touched my chin and turned my face back toward his. His lips were parted, ready to

---

speak, "And it's wonderful, because it's you. You're still Abby Tyndale, the girl I used to know." His touch lingered for a moment too long, his gaze remained on mine, locked, not wanting to look away.

I didn't want to shatter the moment either. Instead of pulling away, I sat there, looking into his eyes. All the feelings that plagued me melted away as he touched me. The lightness in my head made me want to giggle. The idea of his hands on my face, and his lips brushing against mine didn't seem so bad. As soon as the thought entered my head, I closed my eyes. The connection broke. The moment shattered. Jack lowered his hand, and stared out at the sea.

When the moment passed, I realized that I didn't want it to. I realized the truth in Kate's words. I still had the hots for Jack Gray.

CHAPTER TWELVE

I stood in the doorway to Kate's room. Another week had come and gone. Belinda had disappeared again, and the model situation was smoothed over. Or so it seemed. A suitcase sat open on Kate's bed.

Kate was standing in the closet tossing things across the room while she spoke, "I'll be away for a few days. Use the car as much as you want. If something is majorly wrong, call me. I'll be in Brooklyn, so it's not like I'm a million miles away."

My arms were folded over my chest, my shoulder leaning against the doorjamb. "Working over the weekend?"

"Yeah," I heard as she bent over and grabbed a pair of shiny shoes that had four inch heels.

Pushing off the frame, I walked into the room and over to her. When she turned, I grinned, pulling the shoes out of her hands and putting them on the suitcase. "You really expect me to believe that you're working? In these?" I held up a shoe on my index finger. The heel could be used as a weapon, it was so long and pointy. "I'd question your occupation and business associates if I were you. This screams of sexual harassment," I said deadpan. Kate looked like a deer in the headlights. When I couldn't stand it anymore, a smile cracked across my face and I laughed. "Kate! If you're seeing someone, just tell me. Don't pack four times as much clothes just so you can hide lingerie and your fuck-me-heels in the sleeves of your suits." I tossed the shoe back into her pile of clothes.

A sheepish expression washed across her face, as her shoulders squished up around her neck. "I didn't know what to do. I couldn't talk about it with you, and..."

I cut her off, "Why not? If it's something you used to share, and wanted to tell me—tell me."

"Abby, you're not like me," she said as she took a piece of lace from her closet. It was on a hanger so it must have been lingerie, but I had no idea what it'd look like on. It looked more like a napkin with parts missing.

I shrugged, "So. You're not like me." I sat down on the bed as Kate walked over, pulling out the stuff she didn't want from her bag.

"You don't talk about church crap with me, and I don't talk about guys with you. We're both in uncharted waters when it comes to that stuff." She shook her head, making long dark hair fall over her shoulder as she looked into the bag, grabbing another suit jacket and hanging it back up.

"Yeah, we are. Why'd we do that?"

"You've got holy ears," Kate responded, eyes on her suitcase as she repacked.

I laughed, "What? What does that mean!"

"You're a direct line to God and you don't screw around with stuff like that. It's like sticking a fork into a toaster just to see what happens. I might walk around on a daily basis and not think twice about being struck by a lightning bolt, but when I'm standing next to you and doing what I usually do— let's just say I'll think twice about holding an umbrella." At first I wasn't sure if she was serious, but when I didn't hear the laughter in her voice, I knew she meant it.

"Kate! How can you say something like that? It's not like I call the shots. And for the record—no one has died as a result of a lightning bolt to the head while talking trash to me."

Kate snort-laughed, and quickly covered her hand over her mouth to hide it. A grin spread across my face until I couldn't keep my lips shut anymore. Kate sat on the bed and gave me a look. The result was instantaneous. We both broke out into a fit of giggles like we were ten-year-olds, belly-laughing so hard that we couldn't breathe.

When it passed, Kate sat on the bed with the suitcase between us, "So, nothing's off limits? Back to the way things were?"

I nodded, "Hell, yeah. I'm still the same person. I'm not gonna get you killed faster because I got a God badge or something." She grinned at me, but I could still tell she was hesitant. Thinking fast, I wanted to prove it to her. The best way to prove you'd be a good secret-keeper was to offer up a secret, something hidden so deep that you'd never admit to anyone. I cleared my throat, avoiding her gaze, "Besides, talking about guys might be helpful." I spoke the words as I held up a sheer baby doll outfit that was on top of her open bag. The light passed right through it. Kate's eyes were burning a hole in my face. I dropped the garment back into her bag and asked, "What?"

"Abby, what are you saying?" Her voice was soft, concerned. "That you like someone? It's Jack, isn't it? Damn, I was just kidding the other day. I didn't know you really felt that way."

I shrugged, "Neither did I." But after this much time, I had to admit it—I had feelings for him and they weren't going away. It wasn't the remnants of some childhood fantasy. It was real, and made me question everything, every decision I'd made that led me to this point.

"So what do you do? You took vows, right? It's not like you can date him or something?" Kate stopped packing and sat utterly still, watching me.

"No, I can't date him," I answered wistfully. Glancing up at her I added quickly, "And he can't find out. I just... I don't know. I told you because it's bothering me. I see him every day and he's the same boy he used to be, but so much more. He was such a man-whore in high school." I shook my head. "But that doesn't jive with the Jack I see now. Maybe I was wrong about him."

Kate's eyes were huge. She leaned over the bag and grabbed my hand, "What are you saying? That you joined the Nun Run because of him? Holy shit, Abby. You can't be serious?"

I swallowed hard. This was something that I didn't like to admit to myself, and hearing it out loud would cement it in my brain like a tumor waiting to kill me. "Jack was part of the reason." Kate gasped, but fell silent when I continued. "I thought every person had a soulmate—one person that was perfect for them. After high school and four years of college, there was still no trace of that guy. It seemed like he didn't exist, that I didn't get that life. That was the only thing holding me back. I wanted to help people, I wanted to help them find their faith. Life's so damn hard, Kate. It just seemed like the right thing to do, but after everything that's happened, I don't know anymore." My chest felt tight. I think I just admitted to the possibility of more things than I realized were drifting around in my mind.

Kate was shocked into silence. When she recovered, she said, "You've always known which path to take. Your inner-compass is made of titanium, and there is no way in hell that it's broken. Trust your gut, Abby. You always have and it's never led you astray."

"But it is now," I laughed darkly, twisting the bedspread in my hands without realizing I was doing it. "That path was barred shut by the vows. There is no path that includes Jack Gray."

CHAPTER THIRTEEN

Later that night, I pulled open the door to the Galleria. Linda was sitting at the front desk. She beamed at me, "Good evening, Abby. I hope your day went well."

I responded in kind, "It did." Before I could say another word, I heard Jack's voice through the intercom.

"Is she here yet?" he sounded like he was in a bad mood. My heart sank.

Linda pressed the button, and her lips parted to speak, but I leaned in and answered instead, "Be right back."

I pushed through the exterior doors, passing Gus outside, "What's up, Gus? He sounded pissed." I kept walking, turning backwards waiting for an answer.

"The hell if I know!" Gus yelled, his hands flying as he spoke. The tight gait of his walk made me run for the studio.

When I threw open the doors, I saw Jack's foot collide with a can of paint. The contents went flying, lid open, paint splattering as it fell. I stopped in my tracks, as Jack bent forward and pulled his hair in frustration. Every muscle in his body was tightly corded, bulging from beneath his white tee shirt. My jaw dropped, watching him, unable to find my voice. The only other time I'd seen Jack lose his temper was when Belinda showed up.

Setting my purse down on a table, I crossed the massive room. Jack didn't move. He remained bent at the waist, hands clutching his temples. When I was a few paces behind him, my heart was racing. I expected him to turn, but he didn't. Reaching out slowly, I spoke his name at the same time I touched his shoulder, "Jack, what's wrong?"

He jumped out of his skin, rounding on me so fast that I nearly fell over. Gasping for air, his hand clutched his heart, "Abby," he breathed, staring at me like I was insane. "Only you would do something like that. You see everyone else? They ran away!" He screamed the last words, grabbed a bunch of paint brushes and hurled them across the room.

I reached for him again, placing my hand on his forearm before he grabbed something else. When he tried to pull away from me, I held tighter, jerking him back to face me. "Stop. Jack, stop it. Tell me what happened." Jack's dark lashes lowered, looking at my hand on his arm. My heart was racing, beating violently against my ribs. The look he gave me when his blue eyes returned to meet mine made me melt. I started to slide my hand away. It seemed as if I touched him and shouldn't have. The expression on his face was so stormy that I couldn't read him.

"There's nothing to tell, Abby. She managed to get hold of my client list and cancelled all of them, telling them some lies about me." His voice was deep, hushed. He said the words like he couldn't believe it happened.

"And your clients just cancelled?" That didn't sound right.

He nodded, "Yup." His jaw was tight, like he wanted to snap off someone's head. Jack folded his arms across his chest, flexing them, trying to control his anger.

"How'd she get the list?" I asked.

"That's what we were talking about before you got here. Several people suggested it was the new girl." He looked down at me, eyes narrowed, questioning me.

I knew his ex just messed up millions of dollars' worth of work for him, but the question still felt like a slap across the face. Instead of answering, I asked, "And what do you think?"

He shrugged, his voice cold and cruel, "Coulda been. Maybe you're not who I thought. Maybe you're some evangelical nut on a mission to stop pornography and you lumped my studio in with the lot. You're with them, aren't you?"

As he spoke, rage bubbled inside of me. If anyone else had said those words, it wouldn't have hurt so much, but to stand there and hear Jack say them... something snapped inside of me. My hand flew, slapping his cheek so hard that it turned his head. For a moment the only thing I could hear was the slap. My hand fell to my side, stinging like it was on fire. "Fuck you. If that's who you think I am, if

you think I came here to sneak in and destroy you..."
Shaking, I realized that my hands were balled into
fists. I bit my tongue to stop talking, turned on my
heel, snatched up my purse and fled.

By the time I peeled out of the parking lot, my
anger had turned into tears. After a blistering shower,
I threw on a cami and satin shorts. They made me
feel pretty when I felt horrible. I called in a pizza and
threw myself on the couch. Numbness had eventually
taken control of my emotions. Jack's words were like
a sucker punch to my stomach. He blindsided me. I
couldn't believe what he said, even when he was
saying it. The anger that he evoked was something
that I hadn't felt since I left Texas.

The doorbell rang. I pushed myself off the
couch, grabbing Kate's sweater to answer the door.
After wrapping it around me, I pulled the door open.
The only thing I saw was the square white box. A
man was holding it. I didn't look at his face until I
heard his voice, "I was grabbing dinner and I heard
they were taking this to you. I kinda hijacked the
pizza kid." Glancing up, I flinched, seeing Jack
standing on my porch. He continued, "I had to tell
you something... I'm sorry, Abby. I shouldn't have
said that to you. I shouldn't have thought it." I stared
at him through the storm door. Jack looked like I felt.

I didn't open the door. "But you did."

"Aren't you supposed to forgive me?" he asked coyly. His words pissed me off.

"Yeah, but that doesn't mean right now. And it doesn't mean I'm a doormat and ready for more, either." I started to close the door, not looking at him. My throat was so tight I could barely talk. It felt like I'd burst into tears at any moment. I just wanted him to leave.

The smile fell off his face when I answered. As the door closed, Jack pulled open the screen, raising his palm to stop me. Startled, I looked up. There was less than two inches of space between the door and the jamb. Jack's face was so close. He leaned his head on the door frame, "Please don't let things end like this. When you showed up a few weeks ago, I couldn't believe it. It was like fate brought us back together. Since then, I've been ecstatic to see you, hear your voice, and spend time with you. Please. I know I fucked up. I'd give anything to have that moment back and do it over."

His eyes searched mine, waiting for the door to close, but I stood there frozen. It felt like this moment mattered, but I didn't realize how much. I whispered, "Go home, Jack." The door clicked shut, and tears stung my eyes. They finally overflowed and ran down my cheeks.

CHAPTER FOURTEEN

The next morning came and I felt like a train wreck. Sliding on a tank top and shorts, I decided I needed to run and burn off the lingering emotions. I couldn't think straight while I was like this. Sleeping last night didn't happen. I'd tossed and turned, hearing his voice, seeing his face. Jack. The guy haunted me, working his way into my heart like a splinter that wouldn't come out.

Grabbing my keys, I pulled open the front door and stepped outside. My heart sank as the door slammed shut behind me. Stopping abruptly, I saw Jack sat on the bottom step, leaning on the railing. He was wearing the same clothing as yesterday, his dark hair askew, the pizza box next to him on the ground. Frozen, I stood there for a moment. A million thoughts raced through my mind. Pressing my eyes closed, I shook my head wondering if I was an idiot. In the past, asking that very question usually meant I'd moved passed the idiotic line with room to spare. This was another act to add to the list.

"Get off my front porch, Gray," my voice was hard. Jack startled as if he were asleep, and turned to look at me. The expression on his face made me think that everything he said last night was true. He was an ass, saying assy things that he shouldn't have said. Regret rimmed his eyes in dark circles. God he was gorgeous, even when he was sleep deprived, Jack was still stunning. I held out my hand to him, trying to suppress my smile, "Come on. I'll get you some coffee." Jack blinked up at me, before he rose, brushing himself off. He grabbed the pizza box, and followed me inside.

As the coffee brewed, Jack sat at the counter. I felt his eyes on my bare neck, watching me as I moved around Kate's kitchen. "You sleep on people's porches often?"

He shook his head, "Nah, this is new for me. I usually don't mess up that bad." Jack tilted his head, slightly lethargic. "I thought you'd kick me on the way out. Or call the cops last night. Didn't expect this."

I shrugged. "What on earth made you think it was me?" I leaned on the counter across from him. The motion made it feel like my boobs were being thrust into my throat. The sports bra I was wearing smashed me flat, but leaning like that suddenly created super-cleavage. Jack's eyes drifted. I blushed and stood up at the same time he looked away. Neither of us acknowledged it.

He cleared his throat, looking anywhere but at me, "I've gotten a lot of hate mail over the years, mostly from religious freaks who think I'm corrupting America." My stomach turned. The expression on my face must have indicated how I felt about it because he said, "I know, right? Anyway, all fingers pointed at the new girl. Someone had to have passed Belinda my client's names and numbers. Whoever did it played me perfectly."

"So you have a mole. Hmmm." I thought, as the coffee finished. I grabbed two cups and poured.

Handing one to Jack, I said, "Sugar's next to you. I'll grab milk." Turning to the wine fridge, I asked, "Is there anyone at your office that goes back as far as we do?"

Jack shook his head, "No. Everyone else is since college or later. Linda was the obvious person. She controls all the calls and records. No one would even notice if she did it, but she was as upset as I was. Gus was my roommate in college. He helped me get started. He's my business partner. It makes no sense at all. The models don't have access to that stuff, so the only other people are you and the cleaning crew." Silence passed between us. Jack held his cup of black coffee in his hands, staring at me. The look in his eye made me squirm. When he realized what he was doing, his gaze returned to his cup. "I was an ass, Abby."

I smiled weakly, trying to hide how much his words hurt me, "I know. It's part of the package, I suppose."

"What's that mean?"

I shrugged, "Isn't the price of fame supposed to be loneliness? That you can't possibly know who your real friends are, and who's using you?" He nodded. "It's part of the package. Part of being friends with Jonathan Gray."

Jack stood up, and came around the counter. He stood in front of me, looking down at my face. Blue eyes and smooth skin dusted with stubble occupied my gaze. A tendril had come free from my sloppy pony tail while we were talking. Jack's eyes narrowed in on the strands, taking the curl and tucking it behind my ear while he spoke, "I'm not Jonathan Gray, not with you..." his voice was hushed. He said the words and let them hang in the air. "I'll always be Jack. You'll always be Abby."

It felt like I was floating. While his hand touched my hair, gently pressing it behind my ear, his fingers trailed along, down the side of my face and onto my neck. His voice swam in my mind. The butterflies in my stomach wouldn't settle down. They flew in a thousand different directions when Jack touched me. A shiver shook me, making me step back, but the counter was behind me. Jack was in front of me.

His eyes were soft, wanting. They were all over my face and neck, searing a path of heat as they washed over me. "Abby, say something. I need to know what you're thinking." His fingers brushed back the hair again, lightly. The touch nearly made me gasp. The pit of my stomach twisted as heat flushed across my cheeks.

I couldn't tell him what I was thinking. Glancing down, away, I stuttered, "I... I... can't tell you." He had to know he was doing this to me. Didn't he? I didn't know what to do. I was trapped between his body and the cabinets. Time seemed to stop.

Jack's breath washed across my cheek. He lifted his hand, turning my chin back toward him. Blue eyes pierced through me, making me melt. "Why not?" His voice so soft, so seductive. I could feel the reply on my tongue. My heart wanted to say it, but my mind bit back the words. Silence passed between us. We stayed like that, his lips within a breath of mine. When he said, "Tell me, Abby," I could feel the warmth of his breath slide over my mouth. I felt so lost, like I'd been drifting for so long. Jack made me feel found. It took every ounce of restraint not to close the gap between us. I wanted to slide my body into his arms and feel his lips against mine.

Releasing the breath slowly, like it was my last, I said, "I'd like that—Jack and Abby. The way things used to be." Jack watched my lips as I spoke, his dark lashes hooding his eyes. His breath hitched when I spoke, and he froze. Suddenly it felt like a decade ago. We were face to face, a kiss apart from being something more and Jack was frozen again.

But this time, it didn't last more than a second. The warmth that was in his eyes cooled. Jack stepped away from me like he hadn't realized what he'd done. Heat raced across my cheeks. I turned around, facing the counter to hide the blush. Moving slowly, so he didn't notice my hands trembling, I picked up my half-consumed cold coffee and dumped it down the drain. Without turning around, I felt Jack's warmth behind me. I knew he was there. Staring blankly, I told myself not to turn. He placed his cup next to mine, and stepped back. I stared at the black liquid, heart still pounding, drowning out all other sounds.

Jack was leaning on the opposite counter. When I turned around he smiled softly, not holding my gaze for more than a second. I felt insane. Was he toying with me? Did I misread him? I didn't know. I leaned back against my counter, across from Jack.

"So, since I have no clients for a while, let's do something different tonight."

Glancing up at him, I asked, "Like what?"

He shrugged, pushing off the counter, "I'm telling everyone else to take the week off 'til I can sort out who screwed me, so it'll be just me and you. We can do whatever we want. Eat pizza, watch movies, paint... whatever you want."

"Sure. Sounds good."

He turned to leave. I followed him to the door, admiring his sculpted shoulders. Each muscle had a defined curve like he worked out, but I never saw him doing anything. Picturing Jack covered in sweat pushed my pulse higher. I pressed the thoughts back. They needed to be crushed before they messed things up. While I was tripping over my awkward thoughts, Jack turned back and gave me a peck on the cheek.

Grinning he said, "See you later, Tyndale," and tugged my ponytail. He bounded down the steps as I stood there shocked, wondering what the hell just happened.

CHAPTER FIFTEEN

Good God, he made me nuts. I peeled myself off the back of the door after he left and took a cold shower. The rest of the day passed painfully slow. I should have gone back to sleep. Last night sucked so bad that I was lucky if I had a few hours, but I couldn't sleep. I couldn't think. Jack wanted to spend time with me. Just me. He sent everyone else away for an entire week. The giddy girl inside of me wanted to squeal and jump on every bed in the apartment, but I knew I needed to hit her in the head with a brick before she rode off with my brains. I couldn't kiss Jack. It didn't matter that I wanted him. It didn't matter what he did or how I responded. Part of my profession was self-denial. Jack was off limits. I had to stop thinking about him like that.

By nightfall, I convinced myself that I could do it. That we could just be friends. Those feelings would vanish if I commanded them correctly, but I knew nothing about lust or love or like. And that giddy twit inside of me took control the moment I saw Jack. She squealed within me with as much gusto as if I'd given her a unicorn. Why couldn't I control her?

Jack spoke, melting my brain, after dinner, "So, what do you feel like?" He was standing at the counter. The lights in the gallery were switched off, and it felt like we were surrounded by black walls.

Jack asked dangerous questions. I shrugged, like I didn't care—like I was apathetic—trying to hide whatever was causing my mind to malfunction. "I haven't seen the Galleria yet." He looked at me in surprise. "Let's walk through there. Then maybe we can go outside. Play mini golf or something down by the water." That sounded platonic, right? Show me your erotic art and then let's play golf. Sure. Jack smiled at me, grabbing a bottle of wine from the fridge. "Sounds great. But you have to take the tour like a patron. It's the best way to see it." His blue gaze flashed in my direction. I nodded, until I realized what he meant. Jack produced two crystal glasses and poured the wine into each. Handing me one, he said, "Come on."

Refusing to take the glass I said, "Jack, I can't drink that."

"Why not?" He seemed surprised.

"I'm not supposed to drink. You already know that."

"Abby, this is a special occasion. It's part of the experience." He placed the glasses on the counter, before causally leaning his tone body back against it. He tilted his head a little, his hair shifting in the light, "If you don't want to, you don't have to, but it changes things a little bit."

I didn't understand. Eyeing the glass, I asked, "How is slightly intoxicated good? Don't you want people to see what you painted, and not leave with some drunken ambiguous impression in their minds?"

Jack smiled at me like I was cute, cute and maybe a little bit stupid. He turned his head, clearing his throat, saying, "No one gets smashed on half a glass of wine," he laughed. "And it doesn't do what you think. God, haven't you ever had a drink?" I shook my head. I didn't drink, the church used grape juice, and with my dad the way he was, I swore liquor off. All of it. Jack didn't know about my dad. I never told him. Without another word, he seemed to sense he was missing a piece of my story, a piece I wasn't sharing.

He explained, "A little bit of wine is good. A little bit removes preconceptions, apprehensions, and allows you to see what I see. It lets you surrender to yourself a little bit and see things the way I do. For you, a sip or two would be fine. It'd let you see... me." He swallowed hard, like he was offering to reveal something very important.

A chill worked its way up my spine. This was a hard line, something that I said I'd never do, but I wanted to see what he saw. I wanted the chance to get inside his head. It was too tempting to pass up. As I stood there, indecision on my face, a million thoughts racing through my mind, Jack backed away. He didn't hold out my glass again. I moved next to him, and took it in my hands. Pulse pounding in my ears, I lifted the crystal to my lips. The wine slid down my throat with a warm burn. I pressed my lips together, and looked up at him, still holding my glass, wondering if I'd gone insane. "Let's go. Show me what's really happening inside the mind of Jack Gray."

Jack lifted his glass, and turned back, correcting me, "The heart of Jack Gray. Art is always a reflection of the heart, the soul of the painter."

I followed him into the Galleria. It was pitch black. "Wait here," he said and I heard him walk away. The first thing I noticed was a pale blue spotlight slowly growing brighter and brighter on the other side of the room. Music wafted from somewhere. My chest tightened. This seemed romantic, but that had to just be me, right? Patrons didn't come in here and get this taken with Jack. They saw the millionaire Jonathan Gray.

He was back before I could give it more thought. Tilting his head to the side, he said, "Follow me." We walked across the dark space, music slowly drifting through the air. Stopping in front of the illuminated painting he said, "Each canvas will light one at a time. During a show, each patron is given a drink and we follow the lights through the gallery until the last canvas is displayed. Then they all turn on and you can wander around and check stuff out. It makes it more dramatic this way."

My fingernails tapped my glass nervously, "More romantic, too." He arched an eyebrow at me, surprise on his face. Quickly I added, "You know what I mean. You're trying to be evocative here, so don't go giving me the eyebrow. You want your patrons to feel something when they look at the walls. That's what they're buying—the idealized version of Jonathan Gray."

He took my arm and turned me toward the painting. "Maybe, but I want you to tell me what you see. Tell me what you think of Jack, the boy you knew, when you look at these." His voice was soft, as if he were asking a question that could shatter him. One look at his face told me that I could. This made him nervous, but he was excited as well.

Looking at the painting on the wall, I felt my heart clench. It was monochromatic blue, so pale it almost seemed white. The painting was of a woman, nude, showcasing her from the waist up. Her long hair trailed behind her as she danced. Her eyes were closed, a hand by her face another crossed over her breasts. Lifting the wine glass to my lips, I took a sip. My eyes moved across the entire canvas. It was huge. Jack and I fit in front of it, and we could have added ten more people and lined them up shoulder to shoulder—they all would have been able to stand in front of it.

Jack's voice was soft, "What do you see?"

Fear made me reluctant to glance at him. I could feel his gaze on the side of my face, waiting. I didn't want to lie to him, but if this reflected Jack in some way, well, it wasn't something good. I swallowed hard, trying to find the right words. "I see a broken heart. Something lost that haunts you. It's in the colors, the position of the model's body. It's like a million different shades of tears, strewn across a canvas." I breathed hard, worried that I'd offend him. The lights went out, and slowly, a yellow spot light grew brighter across the room. Jack' features were rimmed in light—his smooth skin, the curve of his cheek, the fullness of his lips—they were parted, his eyes watching me, before he put his hand on the small of my back. I repressed the urge to shiver, as he led me across the room.

Stopping in front of a gold painting, he asked, "What do you see, Abby?" his voice was a whisper.

I sipped from the wine first this time. My heart was pounding. This was a lot more intimate that I'd thought. Jack stood next to me, watching me as my eyes slid over the canvas, the wine glass held loosely in his hand. The paint on this one was a myriad of golds with a few highlights of crimson. The model's body was fuller this time. Her soft curves replaced the harsh angles of the last piece. It was sensual, seductive. But there was something else. Where the woman's hand covered her breast, there was a splattering of red. The thick paint was smeared through with soft brush strokes.

"You're still wounded, still mourning someone in this work, but the pain has faded somewhat. The colors, the flow of the composition... it seems like you long to be free, but you can't be. You perceive yourself as trapped. I think people look at this and see the model, and think she's the one who feels that way, but it's not that way at all. It's you, it's Jack who feels the pain and isn't certain what to do. The femininity of it just hides that it's your emotions we're feeling." Glancing at him, I felt bolder, asking, "Am I right?"

I sipped the wine, as he swallowed hard, saying, "More than you know." His eyes lingered on mine. The lightness that was typically there, the playfulness, was gone. Jack was like his painting, open and vulnerable.

The light faded as another turned up. We walked through the gallery, seeing image after image that portrayed a deeply haunted Jack. When we stood before the last canvas, my breath caught in my throat. His hand was on the small of my back, my wine glass nearly empty. Stepping forward, I reached out and touched the paint.

Jack reached for my hand, gently removing my fingers from his work. He didn't let go. "What do you see, Abby?" he breathed.

His hand felt warm on my skin. I didn't know what made me do it. I knew not to touch paintings, but I saw this one and I had to. My fingers were sliding along the woman's face when Jack lifted my hand away and kept it in his. The expression in his eyes was hesitant, like he didn't want to hear what I had to say about this one. I shook my head, "Jack, I don't..." I breathed in, my words trailing off. I didn't want to do this anymore. The rest of his paintings were melancholy, but this one... This one frightened me. It was the white painting, the one of the model the first night I arrived.

Squeezing my hand, he turned me toward him. "Say it. I know you see it. Just say it, Abby." He was so close, his lips were right there. My stomach twisted inside of me. The butterflies and the giddy girl within me scared into silence. The intensity of Jack's gaze made me turn back to the painting. It no longer resembled what we'd made the night it was created. The woman in white was in ecstasy, her long hair moving around her body, caressing it like a lover's hands. Her soft skin, full pale breasts, taut nipples, the curve of her neck, the angle of her head... everything about it made me feel like I couldn't breathe.

"Jack, I..."

"Say it. I see it on your face. I need to hear it fall from your lips. Prove to me you know me. Tell me you see me better than any of the rest. I need to hear it from you, Abby. Tell me." His voice was seductive, demanding, and teasing all at once.

My knees felt weak, my voice caught in my throat. I stared into his eyes with my lips parted, knowing exactly what I saw, but feeling too raw to say it. Lowering my lashes, I closed my eyes and found my voice. "I see it, Jack. Your muse is back. The thing that gave you passion, tormented you, and haunted you is back. You're reeling in ecstasy and dread. It's something you want, but can't ever have. And the one that brings the pain is pure, white as snow... and standing in front of you." The last words were barely audible.

It killed me when I saw it, when my mind snapped the puzzle pieces together. I was the missing muse, the haunting soul that made him feel lost, like he was drifting for over a decade. And that white painting, oh God. I couldn't look at him. I stared into the darkness surrounding us, the last painting still lit.

Jack's grip on my hand loosened. He gently stroked my skin as he leaned in and kissed my temple. Before he pulled away, I felt his breath in my ear, "You see me. Every bit. Every part." When the lights came on, he pulled away. My heart was roaring, flooding my ears with frantic beating. Jack lifted the empty wine glass out of my hands, and put it on the counter. He was tense, the muscle in his jaw tight.

I didn't know what to say. I stood there like a fool, glancing around the room. That painting—it was untouchable sensuality. Loneliness. It wasn't the women I saw anymore when viewing the paintings, it was Jack—his soul bared on every canvas.

CHAPTER SIXTEEN

While Jack turned off the lights, I'd gone outside and sat down on a sand dune. The moon was high, barely giving off any light as it slivered into a new moon. The sound of the waves crashing into the shore calmed me. I didn't know what to think. It felt like I'd done something wrong, something horribly wrong. It was like seeing Jack naked, but much more intimate, and much more damning. When he sat down next to me, I could barely breathe.

Our bodies were an inch apart, close enough to touch, but not. Jack stared at the sea, "That was a lot more intense than I thought it'd be. I'm sorry I made you uncomfortable. I didn't mean to. I didn't expect," he laughed a short high laugh, pushing his hair out of his face and looking at me, "I didn't expect you to do that. No one has ever done that. There are entire books written on what makes me tick, and none of them even came close. But you, Abby, damn," Nervously he ran his fingers through his hair, glancing at me sideways, "you stripped me in a matter of seconds, and saw right through everything. No one's ever done that before. It was wonderful and awful at the same time."

Oh my God. Someone kill me. I couldn't look at him. I didn't mean to make him feel like that. "I'm sorry, Jack. I didn't mean to..."

He bumped into me with his shoulder, cutting off my apology, "Hell no, don't apologize. It was perfect. A moment that was scary as hell, and completely perfect." I glanced at him and he smiled. The tension seemed to fade from his shoulders as the smile drifted across his lips. I smiled back, not knowing what to say, but glad he felt better. "So, tell me. What really happened back in Texas?" Nervous, my eyebrows shot up as I twisted toward him with a *who me?* expression on my face. He laughed, "Yeah, you. If you want to go back, why'd you leave?"

"Now it's my turn to squirm, is that it?" I eyed him half smiling.

"Tell me, Abby. Why are you here?"

Looking at him, I wondered why I felt compelled to spill my guts every time he asked me to. What was wrong with me? It was like I had no sense of self-preservation. I made a face, "I was sent on a forced sabbatical. No warning. No pay. Just good-luck, now get out."

He nearly choked, "Are you serious?" I nodded, "Then why do you want to go back?"

"I have to." I repeated my story in detail, the same one I told Kate about my loans and my contract with the church. "So, if I get through this year, I go back on payroll and I can find another job. If I get canned, my career is over and I'll die from drowning in student loans."

He shook his head, either shocked or appalled. I couldn't tell. I felt his gaze on the side of my face, and turned to look at him. He hesitated for a moment, then asked, "What'd you do? What could have you possibly done?"

More squirming. "Jack, do you really have to know? It was stupid. Stupid enough to get me fired and thrown in jail."

His eyes were wide, "You went to jail?"

I sighed, "Should have. If it were any other job, I would have." Jack looked like he was ready to jump out of his skin if I didn't tell him. I dove into the story and didn't come up for air until I was done. "It was bothering me. All these people pile into the pews week after week and ignore my sermons. I'd just finished a series on helping the poor, but it fell on deaf ears." I sneered without meaning to as I stared into space, "They bought gold plates, pricey Jesus art, and new tapestries. Meanwhile they drive around in big old Caddies with a Jesus fish on their trunks, plowing down poor people at WalMart like they're parking cones. I snapped."

"What'd you do?" he asked.

"I kind of took their lavish stuff and sold it. You know, the communion plates, the flower arrangements, the carved mahogany table that was just like one Jesus might have carved." I rolled my eyes, not looking at Jack. He was completely still. "Basically, I took all their crap and got rid of it. I switched things back to baskets and tin, and gave the money to the poor. I proudly announced what I'd done after the cheap WalMart baskets were passed through the church. People murmured about the gold plates. When I said I sold them there was a collective gasp, until someone asked where the silver ones went." Looking Jack straight in the eye, I said, "They went the way of the gold plates. That nearly caused a mob. The town sheriff was there, getting his holy on, and said it could have been considered theft, but since churches are supposed to give to the poor— and I was their only minister—they couldn't fire me without breaking my contract. Doing that would've meant they had to pay out my contract right then and there before they could shoo me out the door."

"Holy shit, Abby!" he grinned, clearly excited. "You went all Robin Hood on your own church! What'd they do?"

"Yeah, that's where this story goes south. They turned things around one me. They did to me what I did to them. After a few hours of debating in the boardroom, they came up with my sentence. They said if I survived a year on nothing but the grace of God, they'd take me back. There are stipulations in my contract that were put there for other reasons, but they twisted it. So it was walk away and come back in a year, or resign. I can't get another job if they fire me and resigning is just as bad—it shows I didn't have the skill to manage the people entrusted to me. Score one for the rich pew-sitters." I held up my pointer finger and swirled it once in the air, unenthusiastically.

"That's not the same—throwing you out with nothing. That's totally different than you giving their things to the poor," he said it like I didn't realize it. I gave him a look that said I did.

"I realize it's not the same. They still have food, shelter, and money. They didn't pay me enough to have any savings. I have nothing. They kicked me out without a cardboard box. If Kate didn't help me out, things would have been bad. I don't really want to go back, but I'm kind of trapped."

Jack nearly choked. Blue eyes wide, he asked, leaning closer, "You don't want to go back?"

I don't know when it happened, but the idea of going back made me sick. When I left I thought it'd be awesome if I survived the year on their terms. It would really show them what I was made of, but they already knew what I was made of and they didn't like it. They threw me out on my ass because of it.

I shook my head, "No, I don't. Would you want to see Belinda again?" He cringed, "Me neither. They did the same amount of damage; they just gave a different explanation for justification. The thing is, I wonder if I was right. It's been gnawing at me, constantly in the back of my head... I brought this upon myself."

He was quiet, staring at the sand for a moment. Finally he sighed, glancing at me out of the corner of his eye, "So, we both have our futures in the hands of crazy people who don't give a rat's ass."

"So it would seem," I answered staring blindly at the crest of another wave. My stomach turned to lead while I was speaking. It felt like I was being crushed from the inside out. Dread spread through my body, pooling in my stomach, making me nauseous.

Without a word, Jack moved to my feet. Crouching in front of me, I looked at him. He was smiling softly, dark hair messy from the wind. With his hands draped over his knees, he said, "Miss Tyndale, there is one thing I know beyond a shadow of a doubt—you did what was right. There's no mistake about that." I opened my mouth to protest, but he spoke over me, shaking his head. "And to make sure you know, beyond a shadow of a doubt, I'm going to drag you around in the sand until you admit it."

There was no hesitation. Jack reached for my ankles, and pulled hard as he stood up suddenly. I fell back into the sand, my hair trailing behind me. Jack started to walk and I started to scream. With every step he took, sand inched into my pants, shirt, and hair.

I was half-screaming, half-laughing. "Ahh! Stop! Put me down! Sand's going places it shouldn't go!" my voice was shrill. Jack was getting closer to the water. The sand went down the waist of my jeans and was making a sandcastle in my panties. I'd been at the beach when I was a kid and there was always a ton of sand in my swimsuit when I went home, but it was never like this. Dragging me, fully clothed, was forcing enough sand down my pants to fill a sandbox.

Jack was laughing so hard he almost fell over. The muscles in his arms were ripped as he fought to hold onto my kicking legs. "Then say it," he laughed with his hair in his face, beautiful eyes sparkling. "Say you were right or this demonstration ends in the water!" Laughter erupted from him, as he moved faster toward the sea.

Twisting my body, I tried to flip over and kick him to make him let go, but that only filled my bra full of sand, too. "Jack! Put me down!" Pushing off the ground with my hands, I raised my head to avoid a mouth full of sand.

"Say it!" he yelled back, smiling so wide his dimples were showing.

The sand was damp under my hands. Clumps of cold wet grains were being forced into my pants as he pulled. It felt so disgusting that I shrieked, "I was right! I was right! Stop!" Jack dropped my legs in the sand, my feet falling into the surf.

Breathing heavily, he said, "That was really close. I thought you were going in." He was doubled over, hands on his knees grinning ear to ear.

I laid on my back, staring at the sky, laughing, and spitting out sand that had gotten into my mouth. "You suck, you know that?" I laughed, cringing as I felt sand in places sand shouldn't be. "I'm full of sand. All my clothes could be from Sandcastles-R-Us."

He straightened, "Is that so?"

"Which one? The sucking or the sand?" I laughed. I couldn't stop. I hadn't laughed so hard in forever. My sides felt like they were going split open. Before I knew it, Jack was leaning down, reaching for me. I laughed, swatting him away, not realizing what he was doing. He managed to get a hold of my wrist and my thigh. He swung me up over his shoulders while I kicked and screamed.

Jack began to wade into the water, as I pulled his hair trying to stop him. "The sucking or the sand," he murmured, still laughing as he went into the water deeper. When it was up to his knees he spun around and I shrieked. My hair flew out, sand flying as I clawed onto Jack to keep from falling. The more he spun, the dizzier we got. He made it four rotations before losing his footing when a wave knocked him off balance. We toppled over like a drunken totem pole, splashing into the cold water. The salty water filled my clothes and forced clumps of sand out. Gasping, I tried to sit up, but the surf was beating me down.

Jack grabbed my shoulders and pulled me to my feet. Water dripped from his scalp. Inky hair fell across his forehead in clumps of black. Jack pushed a tangle of hair out of my face. "You okay?" The smile was still on his face. I nodded. My shirt clung to every inch of me, revealing how cold I was. I shivered. Jack didn't move. Another wave beat into our legs, nearly knocking me down, but his arms pulled me tightly against him. Jack was tense, every muscle flexed tight, holding me. I splayed my hands on his chest, not looking him in the eye. I thought it would help break the moment, but it didn't. If anything it made it more intense. The curve of his toned body beneath my hands felt perfect. The way his shirt clung to him revealed what he would look like without it.

Jack spoke, his voice deep and alluring. "Were you serious before? You wouldn't go back, if you didn't have to?" Waves pelted at my thighs, making me wobbly. Jack held me tighter, pressing my body closer to his. I raised my hands to his neck to keep from falling over.

The sound of the surf filled my ears. I shook my head slowly. I didn't want to go back. I didn't want to deal with the mess I left behind, but it was so much more than that. Dread filled me, choking me. What if I was wrong? All this time I thought I'd chosen the right path, believed the right things. What if it was all for nothing? I couldn't stomach the thought. Answering slowly, I said, "I don't want to, but I have to. I have to fix it."

"What if I gave you a way to fix it on your own?" his voice was serious, all traces of laughter gone. The surf beat into us, but I couldn't tear my gaze away from his face. The suggestion, his idea, was the beginning and the end. It consumed me in ways I couldn't have imagined. The idea was like Jack in every way—completely tempting and completely forbidden.

CHAPTER SEVENTEEN

I couldn't believe what Jack suggested, but he was serious. I stood there shocked, mute. "Think about it, Abby," was the last thing he said before taking me by the hand and walking up toward the studio.

We were both soaking wet and frozen. He spoke to me, and I answered, but I can't remember any of it. The only thing that kept swimming to the front of my mind was the way his eyes moved over my body. It made me warm, and instead of feeling shy, I wanted more. No one ever looked at me like that—like I was desirable, like I was beautiful. I tried to ignore it, gazing at his broad shoulders as we traipsed through the sand, but that only made it worse. The way his wet clothing clung to his lean figure made me want to touch him, and run my fingers along his tight muscles.

My heart was pounding in my chest as he held open the door for me. I brushed past him, feeling his pecs rub against my bare arm. I repressed a shiver. I've never wanted to stop and hug someone so much in my whole life. But I was kidding myself. I didn't want to hug him. That wasn't enough. I wanted to feel my lips touch his warm chest. I wanted to know what his smooth skin felt like when he had me wrapped in his arms. I wanted to touch him and taste him. I wanted to know every curve of his body, every place that made him moan and say my name.

Completely rattled, I pushed past him. What the hell was wrong with me? I gave this up. I gave him up. Soulmates were important, not this insane wantonness that was bubbling up from somewhere deep inside of me.

Jack missed nothing. Sensing my mood shift, he said, "I didn't mean to offend you, Abby. Maybe I shouldn't have suggested it, but it seemed like a way to free you from your problems. No matter what I do, I'm still trapped—but you. We could fix that. You could pose for me, be a model. No one would recognize you. No one would know it was you. The studio's empty for the next few days. I could make something they've never seen before—something just for you. You could lease it or sell it. You'd be free to do what you want." His voice grew softer as he spoke, eyes locked on mine. "Stay where you want." He sighed, pushing his damp hair out of his face. "It's something I can give you. Something I'd hoped you would have accepted." He paused, adding, "I could pay off that debt for you, but I didn't think you would let me. It seems to be attached to you in a way I don't really understand."

I shook my head. Looking up at his beautiful face, my voice was soft, "No, I wouldn't let you. It was my mistake. I have to pay for it. You're right. It's not like racking up a credit card, it's more than that. That debt symbolizes who I am and what I'll become. Paying it off means I wasn't wrong all these years." Lowering my lashes, I looked away, adding, "And you didn't offend me Jack. It's not..." my throat tightened. I couldn't say it.

Soaking wet, Jack stood in front of me. Tilting my chin up, he asked, "It's not what?" His voice was soft, his hands warm. Closing my eyes, I pulled my chin back. He released me.

"It's just not a good idea, not with the other paintings the way they are." I felt so hot, but my skin was freezing. Why was he making me say this? But Jack's face was still, waiting for an explanation. I stammered the words out, fumbling my fingers as I spoke, nervously looking everywhere except at Jack's eyes, "Not with me."

He nodded once, arms folded across his broad chest, shirt clinging to his skin. "Don't do that, Abby. Don't act like I can't handle it. I wouldn't have offered if I thought I wouldn't be able to do it. There's no touching, and I don't date the models. You'd be the model, Abby. We're both adults, and I don't think either of us wants to flush our reputation away."

My stomach was twisting in knots as he gazed at me. Finally he asked, "If the debt was gone, what would you do? Would you continue working as a minster somewhere? Or would you do something else? Start over?"

The pit of my stomach fell. It was the question that I dreaded, the one that plagued me at night. If I said I'd start over, that was total failure. And not just failure, like I chose the wrong career—it was failure that would crush my faith. It would destroy my life, who I was, everything I did—it would have been for nothing. Pressing my lips together, I tilted my head, eyes looking away from him as I said, "I'd find another congregation—get transferred. There would be more places that could take me without that debt hanging over my head. I don't think I'd start over again." As I spoke the last words, they felt barbed. I was certain he heard, *I wouldn't choose you.*

His shoulders stiffened as I spoke. "Then let me do this for you, Abby." His eyes shone like twin gems, earnest and pleading. He was offering me freedom. My curiosity didn't dismiss his suggestion yet.

"I don't think I can, Jack. But, what would it look like? Would it be like Cheri's painting?" My heart hammered in my chest.

Jack smiled softly. "Come here," he held out his hand and I took it. He led me through the studio to a full length mirror and flipped on the light. "It wouldn't be like Cheri's painting. It would be yours— the only Jonathon Gray masterpiece that was in full color. Everything else is muted, like ghosts whispering from the past. But you, your painting would be vibrant and stunning. It would reflect you, how I see you. What I want for you..." his voice softened as he looked at me in the glass from behind my shoulder.

"I'd paint you from here," he placed his fingers gently on my waist and slowly dragged them up my side, passing over the curve of my waist to the side of my breast, touching my shoulder gently, and ending his caress on my cheek, "to here." My shirt clung to my body, revealing everything. As his fingers moved it felt like someone dropped an anvil on my chest, and breathing became difficult. Jack's eyes watched me in the mirror, his hand sliding along my side, grazing my body. When he first turned me toward the mirror, I nearly died. I had no idea he could see so much through the wet clothing. I wasn't even wearing white. It didn't seem to matter.

He added, "There's a skirt that would cover your lower half. It's not a full nude, and it's nothing like Cheri's. It'll be so much more." His lips were by my ear as his breath warmed my neck.

Staring in the mirror, my heart slammed into the side of my ribs, jerking wildly when he touched me. My lips burned. I wanted to feel his kiss, know his taste. That's when I could see it. He wasn't the issue here. It was me. I couldn't pose for him because he was making me such a mess. Jack barely touched me and I melted. Everything about him was making me crazy. Even looking at me in the mirror, his gaze was different than mine. A horrible realization flooded me.

"Jack?" His eyes had been drifting across the reflection. They snapped back to my face when I said his name. "Am I shadow and light? Curves and lines?" I forced the question out. I had to know. What was he looking at when he saw me—a woman or a piece of art?

His hand traced my cheek. Tilting my head to the side, I extended my neck, feeling his fingers slide over my skin. "Of course you are," he smiled deeply not realizing that his words shattered me. My stomach sank, landing in my toes. I couldn't breathe. All this time he was looking at me, I thought he wanted me. I thought the feelings were mutual, but Jack was being Jack. I was his muse, but there was nothing more.

He added, "I've always wanted to paint you. Every line, every curve flows through your body with such clarity. It's like you were formed to inspire." As he spoke, his gaze drifted over my wet shirt, down to my waist.

"You'll conceal my identity?" I asked, and he nodded. If he'd said anything else, I would have said no, but the look on his face and the tone of his voice... I was nothing but shadows and light to him—

a grouping of lines that made a nice shape. It didn't matter if he saw me, painted me, or touched me. Jack didn't see bare skin. Jack didn't want to trail his lips over mine. He never did. I don't know why I said it. Maybe it was because people do stupid things after 2:00am, maybe it was because it cemented what he thought of me and allowed me to get over him. Damn, fifteen years passed and I was still hung up on a guy who didn't want me. I was so messed up.

Looking him in the eye, I nodded, saying, "Okay, but let me take a shower first." I stepped away from the mirror, Jack shocked into silence behind me. It took him a moment to realize what I said.

He beamed in disbelief, "You'll do it? Really?" He sounded giddy. It crushed me. His enthusiasm stomped me into the ground. How did I mistake that for something else?

I nodded, pulling my cold shirt off my skin as I walked, remembering the old adage, *Nothing good happens after 2:00am*, and totally blowing it off.

CHAPTER EIGHTEEN

I stood in the studio shower with hot water pelting me for way too long. The sea was freezing. It didn't matter what time of the year it was, the water was always cold. As I rinsed off, more sand piled around my feet. I'd be shampooing sand out of my hair for days. Determination flowed over me as I dried off. This would help me kick my lusting after Jack. And I was curious what the painting would look like. Every other piece he had hanging in the gallery was muted, like a distant memory, soft and faded. I was his muse, and I was here. I shook my head, padding out of the studio shower barefoot. The cement floor was cold under my feet.

"Jack?" I called when I didn't see him. A large roll of canvas had been spread out. There were streaks of orange and yellow across it. He'd started. It was already different than what he normally did. I padded toward the canvas, keeping my dripping hair from leaving drops of water on it.

A door opened and Jack walked through. My fingers clutched my towel tightly. The bravado that I'd mustered before must have been washed away, because I felt naked and I was holding a towel. "Abby," he smiled walking toward me, holding several cans of paint. "You ready?" I nodded since I didn't trust my voice. I smiled back at him with a confidence that I didn't feel.

After putting down the cans, Jack pointed at the stool with a paint brush in his hand and another between his teeth, "Sit." He popped open the tops of several cans and stirred while I walked toward the stool like it was the chair. Staring, I stepped toward it slowly, like it was going to kill me. But I didn't stop. It was like a moth flying into a flame after its wings caught fire.

I sat on the stool, the towel still gripped in my hand. The hem of the towel was short and when I sat, it climbed up showing all of my thigh. Nervously, I pressed my lips together. Jack had a brush behind his ear, one in his mouth, and several in his pockets. He gave me one look and said reassuringly, "Don't be nervous Abby. I won't touch you." Like that would calm me. He stared at my white knuckles, gripping the towel like I'd die if I let it go.

I breathed, "I know you won't." His eyes were so blue, so full of life. It was hard to not be filled with his happiness when he was like this, but the thought of dropping the towel only made me grip it tighter.

"Then what's the matter?" he asked seriously. "There's no one else here. I was watching you in the mirror before, and you seemed okay with it. It'll be easier than that, Abby." Without meaning to, I blushed. The burn intensified as he spoke, making him grin wider. "Um, Abby. Can I ask you something?" he said shyly. I nodded, too tense to talk. "Have you done this before?"

Surprised he asked, I said, "No. This moment of insanity will only be once, thank you."

He laughed, clarifying, "I didn't mean it like that. I meant, has anyone seen you before? You know, before you got all churchy—you had to have been with someone?" his voice trailed off, the question hanging in the air. The question that I didn't want to answer, but he could read it on my face. No. No one had seen me. I'd been alone all this time.

His back straightened, "Oh. Oh, God, really? You've never… ?" he trailed off, not asking the rest of the question when I glared at him. The only one I ever wanted was him. How could he ask me that? It seemed cruel. "Maybe we shouldn't..." but before he finished speaking, I dropped the towel.

My voice was steady, "Maybe we should. Paint me, Jack. Make me a Jonathan Gray girl." I stared straight ahead, feeling his eyes on my bare skin. Controlling my blush, I forced it back. The towel draped over my lap, and I clasped my hands together on top of it, like I was waiting for a bus and walked around naked in front of hot guys all the time.

Jack didn't speak again for a while. He moved quickly and carefully, putting his brushes where he needed them. He went to work dabbing thick cold paint on my torso, along the curve of my waist in long strokes. His eyes darted back and forth as he worked, seeing me without seeing me. I thought I could handle it until his soft brushes were stroking paint onto my lower ribcage.

Without looking at me, Jack asked, "Can you rest your arms on top of your head for a while? I need to make sure your breasts don't touch the paint on your chest."

His words knocked the air out of my lungs. Roughly I sucked in a breath, and he stopped to look up at me. His face was so close. I could smell the ocean in his clean hair. Bits of dark hair seemed to curl as it dried. "Abby," he breathed, staring at me like he was drinking me in. But he wasn't. He was waiting. "Lift your arms." I did as he asked, the towel sliding out of my lap.

Pressing my eyes closed, I concentrated on the frantic pace of my heart. There wasn't a scrap of clothing on me. Jack could see every inch of me. The soft bristles on my skin fanned out the thick paint, smoothing it. Jack was working the paint differently than he usually did, spreading vibrant colors from my waist toward my neck. When the brush stroked along under my breast, I couldn't stand it. Fighting the urge to squirm in my chair, I opened my eyes and stared straight ahead. But it didn't help. Now I could see Jack, his eyes narrow as he concentrated, his brush dipping in cobalt paint, dripping on my lap as he stroked the cold paint across my naked body. Stroke by stroke he covered my breasts, each stroke of blue brighter than the last. When the brush slid over my nipple, I couldn't hold myself still. I squirmed, a gasp rushing from my lips.

Jack stopped, and gazed at me, "Are you all right? I should have said something. The paint's cold and the skin's more sensitive there." I nodded, too nervous to speak. Jack's lips, his face was in front of my breast. As he spoke, his warm breath slid over the painted skin, making me shiver. I pressed my eyes closed, trying to ignore the erotic images flashing through my mind—all involving Jack. "Should I stop?" he asked.

Flicking my eyes open, hands still draped over my head, I said, "No. I'm fine." Jack eyed me for a moment. He must have decided that I was telling the truth. His paintbrush dipped back into three different cans and returned to my breast. Each stroke swept from beneath my breast, passing over my taut nipples and onto the top of my breast. My eyes were mashed shut like he was torturing me. Grabbing my wrists, I held onto my arms tightly on top of my scalp, digging my nails into my skin so I'd sit still. Jack's hands were controlling the brushes, spreading out the paint. Soon the cool wet strokes were replaced with soft dry brushes, fanning the paint. I squeezed my thighs tighter, trying to ignore the sensations he was sending through my body.

After the last stroke, I heard his voice and opened my eyes. He stood in front of me, admiring the paint clinging to my naked body. His voice was rough, "Damn, Abby, you're beautiful." He breathed the last word, like he couldn't believe what he was seeing.

I stared at the dark stubble on his cheeks, the hair that fell into his eyes. Jack was still Jack and I was nearly undone by strokes of his paint brush. "You ready?" he asked.

I nodded, "As ready as I'll ever be." My voice was higher than usual, tight. My knees were shaking from holding my thighs together, my arms burned from keeping them above my head for so long.

"You look perfect. Don't move. Not yet." He turned his head abruptly, and grabbed a huge crinoline skirt from the other side of the studio. When he came back to the chair, he untied the thing and said, "Stand."

That was easier said than done. My legs shook as I slid off the stool. My balance was questionable when I wasn't naked with my arms pinned to the top of my head. Jack smiled briefly as I gained my footing. His hand brushed my elbow, steadying me, shooting dark currents through my stomach more intensely than I thought possible.

Leaning forward, Jack opened the huge skirt so that it was a flat panel. He held it by two strings and moved closer to me. Reaching around behind my back, careful not to touch me, he pulled the skirt around my waist. As he tied it, he looked down at me, every curve exposed, his lips inches away. After the bow was tied, I felt a little better. Jack touched the crinoline skirt, holding my hips and giving me a little push for the canvas. I moved toward it, my throat tight.

"What are we doing Jack? I can't lay down on it without putting my arms down."

"Keep your arms up, Abby. I still have to paint your hair, too. But we're doing it different this time. I'll lay you on the canvas. You rest your hands high, away from your body. I'll fan your hair and paint it while you lay there. Then I'll shoot you with the overhead camera; then I'll paint. Okay?" I nodded. "Okay, step over here and face away from me. This is going to be like the trust game, but it'll feel worse."

"Because I'm naked, covered in paint, and holding my arms over my head? Or because you're going to drop me?" I grinned. He couldn't see me, and I suddenly felt a little more confident.

"Wise ass," there was laughter in his voice.

"We should do this with you when I'm done. I'll catch you, Jack. I totally promise."

To my surprise, he said, "Anything you want, Abby." He cleared his throat, his tone changing again. "Keep your hands over your head, and lean back. I'll catch you before you hit the floor."

Nodding, I fully intended to do it. This was the easiest part of the whole thing, but I stood there unable to move. Every time I thought I could lean back, I froze and didn't move. Finally Jack asked, "How the hell did you let me paint you if you don't trust me?"

I shrugged, "I'm mental, Jack. You know that. I sucked at this game when I was little."

His voice was deep, alluring, "You're not little anymore, Abby. Fall. Do it. I'll catch you." His voice was firm, commanding. It did something to me. I closed my eyes and leaned back. My body tensed as I fought the natural instinct to curl into a ball and try to stop the fall. I didn't flare out my hands to stop me, they stayed clung to my head. The air rushed by, making the paint feel colder when Jack's warm hands caught my shoulders and slowly lowered me to the floor.

He smiled softly at me, upside-down, "I'll always catch you, Abby." He didn't say anything else. The focused expression overtook his features again. He worked, stroking out my hair, covering it in paint, and painting the surrounding canvas. His eyes slid over my body several times when he was done with my hair, arms folded, a finger tapping his lips. Every breath I took made my chest expand and my heart beat harder. Jack tapped, and I couldn't move. After a moment, he grabbed more paint and started painting the skirt I was wearing. The paint soaked in making it heavier. His fingers wrapped around my ankle, moving my legs farther apart.

"Jack," I breathed his name without meaning to, my eyes closed, skin still tingling where he touched me.

I heard him jump to his feet as he said, "Stay like that. Don't move." Within seconds I heard the shutter of the camera snapping away. Then he was back, standing over the canvas, looking down at me. "Abby." I opened my eyes, glancing at him without turning my head. I flushed. He smiled, not commenting on it. "Can you do this?" He moved his hand, pointing at mine, asking me to copy him. I did as directed, smearing the paint beneath my arm. I moved my head from side to side, dragging my hair, making it look like a tangle of tendrils on the fabric. Finally he said, "Roll over very slowly. Don't press your side to the canvas. Just try to flip over like a pancake the best you can."

I arched an eyebrow at him. "Pancakes don't wear floor-length tutus. I don't know if I can, Jack. I don't want to mess it up."

"You can't mess it up, Abby. Flip." He sounded certain.

"And my arms? You still want them above my head?"

He nodded, serious. His eyes were on me, moving across my body, taking in each and every curve covered in paint. "I want the impression of your breasts, your stomach, and your waist." His finger was tapping his lip, that perfectly pink lip.

Tearing my gaze from him, I did as he asked. I attempted to flip over onto my stomach. The sensation of the paint sliding made the landing feel different than I thought. I expected it to feel like a belly flop, which would have stung my stomach and breasts, but this felt different. The paint slid as my weight came down, pressing my figure into the canvas.

My body let out a huff of air, paint covered hair trailing behind me, sticking to my back as I flipped.

The skirt was huge and half twisted, half folded under me. "Oh, Jack, I'm sorry. The skirt..." I was about to apologize, but I felt his hands under my arms pulling me backwards, away from the canvas like a stamp. My back was to his front, as he lifted me. The skirt sounded like a million shopping bags crinkling at the same time. He twisted me toward him.

Eyes dark, he pressed his body against mine, getting paint all over his shirt. "The painting is perfect because you are perfect. Abby..." his voice hitched in his throat. His arms were wrapped around my waist, his lips next to my ear, silent.

My heart was racing in my chest. Jack held onto me, naked and covered in paint. Before my bubble could swell any bigger, it burst. Jack's arms loosened, releasing me. He nodded toward the shower and said, "Better change."

CHAPTER NINETEEN

After the shower, I put on a pair of Jack's sweats and laid on the couch in the studio. Jack continued to work as I drifted off to sleep. A strange feeling spread over me before that night was over. I didn't know if it was dread or elation, but somewhere in my gut I knew it was both.

I woke up the next morning to the scent of coffee and Jack's painting hung on the wall. He stood in front of it, freshly dressed, dark jeans hugging his narrow hips, shirtless. His feet were bare as well. Laying on my side, I stared at what I'd done. It was so different from his other paintings. The oranges and blues were bright, passionate. There was nothing muted about it. Turning, Jack saw my eyes, and smiled.

He walked toward me, with a cup of coffee in his hand, "Good morning," he said, handing it to me. I sat up, reddish brown hair pressed to the side of my face.

He looked stunning. I forced my eyes to his face and smiled shyly, "Good morning Jack." I jumped in the shower and put on another pair of his sweats. When I came out, Jack was standing there, waiting for me.

There was a moment of silence as my eyes drifted past him to the canvas. That's when he asked softly, "Do you regret it?"

I glanced up at him, and shook my head. "No. Necessary evil, I suppose."

He bristled, "Of course." Reaching for his shirt, he turned and pulled it over his head. The black tee molded to his body, as he walked away.

It took me a second to figure out what upset him. "Jack," my voice was sharp. "I'm a minister and

I stripped for you. There's a naked painting of me hanging on your wall." My voice cracked. The wave of what-have-I-done crashed into me.

He turned back to me, a wounded expression on his face. "It's not stripping. It's not hooking. It's not fucking like that!" The veins in his neck rose as he yelled.

"Maybe for you it wasn't, but for me it was." He huffed, and turned, ready to leave, but I grabbed his arm. "Stop, and listen. Damn it, Jack! You don't listen! Maybe it meant nothing to you, but it did to me. It matters. This is something that was supposed to be with my soulmate, and not strewn across a canvas. I wanted the first man to see me, the first guy that touched me, to be someone who actually loved me. I wanted those things, Jack. This isn't how I thought things would be. It feels wrong, not because of you, but because of me." My voice faded as I spoke. I couldn't look at him. It wasn't shame; it was disappointment. Somewhere in the back of my mind, it felt like I settled, and it unhinged me.

Jack stood in front of me, his jaw set tight, listening. When I stopped, he breathed deeply, trying to calm himself. "What do you want, Abby?" His voice softened. He leaned closer to me. I took a step back. "Do you want me to tell you what you want to hear? I don't even know what the fuck that is? I try to talk to you, to tell you, but you seem so unattainable... like a goddess just out of reach. Last night it was all I could manage to keep my hands off of you. The scent of your skin was intoxicating, and yet, I couldn't touch you. I can't ever touch you. I can't ever have you; I can't ever love you because you're not mine. You're out of bounds."

My voice squeaked, my jaw dropped as I looked up into his stormy eyes, "What did you say?"

His shoulders slumped as he shook his head, his hands pressing on his temples. "You're out of bounds. I can't be the one that makes you fall, Abby. You chose your path, you said your vows, and since that's the life you want, I'll help you keep it." He turned from me, walking back to the painting.

I stared at his back. Every part of me felt like it shattered into a million pieces. Did he say he loved me? Did I really hear those words fall from his gorgeous lips? Padding to him slowly, I stopped behind him, asking, "Jack?" He turned, his expression still unpredictable. "Kiss me." I whispered the words, standing there in front of him with my lips parted, barely breathing.

His eyes fixated on my lips, watching me, wanting me. Without tearing his gaze away, he said,

"I can't. I can't do that to you. I missed my chance." The last words were a whisper. I stepped closer to him, looking up into his face. He was close enough to touch, but I didn't dare.

"What chance?" I asked.

He gazed down at me, blinking like it would erase the memory from his mind. "High school. Before you ran. I didn't want to mess things up between us. I thought if you really wanted to kiss me that you'd complete the kiss. But you didn't."

"I thought you didn't want me. From the way you acted, I thought I didn't matter to you like that."

His eyes were wide, and soft, so soft. He breathed, "I've always wanted you like that. But the things you said, about my past, about the other girls—it seemed to cancel out any chance with you."

Swallowing hard, I gazed at his face, his eyes that seemed so lost and haunted. I shook my head softly. "I grew up, Jack. Your past doesn't matter to me. It's part of you."

He reached out for me, tugging me by the waist closer to him. Gazing down into my face, he whispered, "I'm sorry, but I can't be the one to start this. I can't be the one to pull you from your calling and break your vows."

Reaching up, I stroked his cheek, gently running my fingers along his smooth skin. He sucked in a jagged breath, closing his eyes. Jack's scent was perfect, filling my head, making me bold. Leaning in, I pressed my lips gently to his. Lowering my lashes, I could feel his breath hitch as it happened. My head swam. The sensations flooded my body making me want more of him, but he pulled away.

"I can't, Abby..." He pressed his lips together tight, looking away from me at the canvas on the wall. "I can be anything and everything else for you, but I can't be the one who makes you fall."

CHAPTER TWENTY

The next few days passed in silence. I went back to Kate's to get away from Jack, but it did me no good. Everything made me think of him. The way his eyes looked at me the other night. The way he spoke of me as though I was an angel and his love would condemn me made me cry.

Kate noticed I was missing Sunday night, and grilled me on it the next day. Her dirty mind asked, "Did you sleep with him? Why'd you stay over?"

Swallowing hard, I picked at my bagel. I wanted to talk about it with someone. Jack held me so high that it felt like I was horrible for wanting him so much. I glanced up at her, "He painted me."

She choked on her bagel. "What? Like one of his naked girls?"

"Exactly like one of his naked girls," picking at the bread, I formed a pattern on my plate. I pushed the crumbs around with my finger. Glancing up, I could see Kate's eyes widen.

"Abby," she stared, not blinking, paused like a cartoon character in total shock. "Why? Why would you do that?"

"He's giving me the painting. I can do what I want with it. No one can see it, and it can stay at the top of my closet forever or I can auction it off and get rid of my loans. It would let me start preaching somewhere else."

"Who in their right mind will take a nude preacher? Abby, what were you thinking?"

I glared at her, wishing she asked different questions. "You won't be able to tell it's me, and no one else was there, so they won't know who it was either. Kate, it's already done. I didn't have a problem with it, so neither should you."

"Then what's wrong?" she sipped her coffee, her tone softer.

"He said he loves me." My eyes stung and I could feel my lashes growing wet as I tried to stop the tears. I was such a mess. Before I left Texas I knew exactly what I wanted, and now, the only thing I wanted was Jack and he wouldn't have me.

"Abby," she gasped, "what happened? What'd you say?"

"I tried to kiss him, but he wouldn't. He said he would be the reason I "fell." Kate, he talks about me like I'm an angel, and being with him will ruin me. After all this time, I found out why he didn't kiss me, that he loved me since the beginning. And now it's too late." Kate shifted her chair so she was sitting next to me, and handed me a napkin to dab my eyes. I took a deep breath to steady myself.

"There's only one thing to do, Abby." I glanced at Kate. Her dark hair was swooped up into a sloppy ponytail on top of her head, and an oversized sweater swallowed her body. "You need to show him that you've already fallen."

CHAPTER TWENTY-ONE

Kate continued, "If he thinks you're out of reach, if being with you will hurt you, he won't do it. You have to show him that it won't, Abby. Make him see you, all of you—your heart, mind, and soul—and accept that you choose him."

I shook my head, "I tried, Kate, but he wouldn't listen. He pushed me away."

"Was this before or after he painted you?" she asked, a sharp gleam in her eye like she had a plan.

"After," I replied, eyeing her. "What difference does that make?"

"It's a world of difference. Here's what you should do," and she started telling me a plan that made me blush brightly. Kate laughed, shaking her head. "It's an all or nothing plan. You have to be bold. Shyness will only make him think he's corrupting you. Do you think you can do it?"

"I have to try."

––––––––––––

Only a few short weeks had passed since I got here. I managed to pay my loans once by myself and it felt good. I felt good. Part of me that had been repressed suddenly felt alive, and she wasn't backing down without a fight. Jack was the prize and I couldn't lose him again.

I spent the rest of the day getting ready. I washed my hair way too many times, until the sand was all gone. There was a small beach in the drainpipe by the time I was done. I pulled on a lacey bra and panty set that I got at the mall a few days ago. I bought them thinking no one would ever see them. Now I was putting them on hoping that Jack would see them and take them off of me. Butterflies swarmed in my stomach, making me feel sick. Part of me whispered that I should embrace the sickness and bury myself under the covers, but my giddy inner child was ready for an adventure. She wanted to jump off cliffs, and do things that made my heart pound. We high-fived and I shoved her into the back of my mind where she tied up my reasoning and held it captive with her unicorn. There was no way I would chicken out. I was going to do this.

After gazing in the mirror, I slid a pair of dark jeans over the sexy bottoms and felt beautiful. My hair cooperated, my makeup looked exceptional. There was only one thing left to do. I grabbed my bag and headed toward Jack's studio.

When I arrived the place was dark. I let myself in, and locked the door behind me. Walking through the blackened halls, I looked for Jack. The echo of my heels hitting the tile filled my ears. Moving through the space, I found Jack outside, behind the studio, sitting in a chair with a drink in his hand, staring up at the sky.

"Hey," I said after watching him for a moment. His dark hair fell forward as he lifted his head and looked at me.

His face lit up, "Abby. I didn't think you were coming tonight."

I shrugged, like what else would I be doing. My heart beat wildly in my chest as I straddled the chair next to him and said, "I heard you were short on models. I want another painting, but I want to help paint it."

His eyes were dark and brooding. They slid over my face, hesitant to go lower. "I barely survived last night. I don't have it in me, Abby."

Standing, I said, "I think you do." I pulled him up by his hand and led him back inside. Removing his drink from his hand, I put it down on the table. Leaning into him, I spoke softly, but firmly, "I'll be clothed this time, Jack. You can do it. I won't let you say no."

Jack's eyes met mine. He seemed so distraught. "I already told you, Abby. I can't do this. I can't undo you. You're out of reach for me. You always have been."

I took his hand in mine, and pressed it over my heart. His fingers grazed my breast, "Do you feel what you do to me?" If my heart slammed into my ribs any harder, they'd crack. He could feel it, racing wildly beneath his hand. His gaze remained melancholy. "Jack, look at me." His blue eyes met mine. They were darkening, wanting something he couldn't have. Holding his hand to my heart, I leaned in to kiss him, but he looked down.

His voice was breathy, barely controlled, "I can't. Abby, I can't make you fall."

"Jack," I cupped his face in my hands, pulling it back up so I could look into his eyes. "I've already fallen. Nothing you do will stop that. Pushing me away only makes us both miserable. Paint me." I whispered, pressing my chest to his, feeling the warmth of his body against mine. Before he could say no, I stepped away. Peeling off my shirt as I walked, I grabbed a brush and a can of paint. Jack's eyes burned into me, I felt hot all over, my stomach twisting in knots. I dipped the large brush in red and drew a long stroke between my breasts over my lace bra. The color clung to the fabric, seeping beneath it.

I dipped the brush again and again, putting on more colors and painting my upper body. Jack watched me, frozen, his jaw tense, arms folded like he was holding himself back. I didn't stop. I ignored his warning. Dropping the brush, I allowed it to splatter on the floor at my feet. Lowering my hands, I slowly unbuttoned my jeans, sliding them down over the curve of my hips, revealing the white lace beneath.

Jack's eyes locked on mine. They were pleading for me to stop, his voice was heavy with want, warning me, "Abby..." His voice was ragged, his breathing tight. His eyes watched me like he needed me, wanted me.

The jeans slipped off my ankle and I stepped out of them, bending over slowly, showing him the curve of my hips. I pushed the denim aside. I dipped my hands in paint, rising, and watching him. Ribbons of red and blue trailed up to my elbows as I held my hands in front of me. Sliding my fingers across my body, I slowly covered every curve in blue and red, painting over my pretty lace set without a second thought. Jack's eyes watched me like a predator ready to pounce. The muscles in his arms twitched.

Breathlessly, I asked, "Which canvas?" There were several clean canvases laid out on the floor. Jack unfolded his arms for half a second and pointed. I followed his finger to the largest one in the center of the room. Moonlight spilled in through the window behind Jack, making him look ethereal. I stood in front of the canvas and glanced at him, my heart pounding in my chest. I barely had a voice, "Help me lay down. Jack..." I whispered his name, feeling it form on my swollen lips. Every part of my body was tingling, wanting him to touch me, to taste me.

For a moment he didn't move. His eyes remained on my body, refusing to look in my eyes. Slowly, he pushed off the table he was leaning against as he had watched me cover my flesh in paint. He moved slowly, and stopped in front of me.

Heart pounding in my chest, I asked, "Help me fall, Jack," and before he could answer I leaned back. Without a moment's hesitation, Jack reached for me. His strong arms caught my body, linking around my waist, and pulling me back up toward him.

He was breathing hard, "Abby, you undo me. How could I tell you no when you act like that?"

Jack turned me toward him, his firm hands pressed into the soft skin at my back. "Then kiss me. Show me you love me."

He hesitated, "What about your vows? What about...?"

"You're the one person that's perfect for me. As long as you know it, I trust you."

"There's no going back, Abby." He closed his eyes, trying to speak—his body pressed into me, hard and wanting. Warmth covered my skin like fire, racing to my core.

"There was never anything without you." I linked my arms around his neck and pressed my body flush to his, as I lightly dusted my lips across his mouth.

Jack melted in my hands. The wall that he put between us came crashing down. I gasped as he pulled me tightly against him, his lips pressing harder against mine, tasting me, testing me. His hands slid up and down my body, feeling the curves of my bare waist, sliding over the thin fabric that covered my butt. Paint covered his hands as he threaded them through my hair, his kisses becoming hotter.

Without a word, he swept me up in his arms and lowered me to the canvas. Covering my body in kisses, he pulled back, his face covered in paint, like mine. I smiled at him as he took the can of red and drizzled the paint across my chest. Placing the can down, he took the blue and poured it over my stomach. The paint was cool to the touch, sliding over my hot skin more sensually than the night before. Jack put his hands on me, stroking the paint with his fingers, with my body moving under his touch. Sighing deeply, my head was swimming. Jack pulled his shirt over his head, and removed his jeans. My eyes slipped over his body, wanting to touch it, taste it, and feel him inside me.

Jack laid himself on top of me, slowly sliding against me, paint spreading, mixing between us. He rolled off of me, and pulled me on top of him. Straddling his naked hips, I looked down at him, paint dripping from my hair. His hands reached up behind me, unclasping the once white bra. It fell away, and he cupped my breast in his hand, squeezing me gently. I leaned my head back, swaying. My hips began to move on their own as he touched me, making me moan his name.

Every spot on my skin was on fire. I wanted his hands, his lips, touching me, kissing me. I writhed under his touch, craving more, not feeling sated. Calling his name, I tried to pull him to me, but he whispered, "Not yet," in my ear. Teasing me with his teeth, he nipped my neck and trailed kissed down my body, stopping at my panties. Lifting my bottom, he slid his hands underneath and pulled them off, tossing them aside.

I knew the paint could cover every inch of our bodies and wash away, but when his lips trailed over my painted neck I wondered. As if Jack could read the thoughts running through my mind about the paint, he said, "It tastes like sugar, sweet like syrup. The paint can't hurt you, Abby." I gazed at him, elated. That was part of my plan that had been uncertain. I'd planned on trying to drag him back to the shower, but when his paint covered lips began to kiss me, my brain melted.

Pulse pounding in my ears, I trembled as Jack's hand traveled up my thigh and slid between my legs. His lips brushed kisses on my neck, as his fingers moved inside of me. Jack's eyes closed as he felt me, his breath ragged, "Abby.. ." He breathed in my ear, lowering his body to mine, keeping his hand between my legs, rubbing, stroking me gently. My back arched off the canvas, pushing into his hand harder. I needed him, wanted him. I called his name again, softly saying it over and over. He answered, "Tell me you want me, Abby. Tell me to take you and make you mine." I could feel his beautiful smile against the side of my face.

I could barely breathe. Jack pulled his hand away, sliding it between my breasts, circling the nipple with my wetness. Bending down he blew gently, making me shiver, before putting his warm mouth on my body. Trailing his tongue along the soft flesh, he licked and sucked, making me long for him even more.

Over and over I moaned softly, "Make me yours, Jack. Please. Take me." My nails dragged across his skin when I couldn't take it anymore. I would have done anything he wanted in that moment just to feel him inside of me. That was when Jack moved on top of me. He was so hard, his length pressing against me, sliding himself between my legs and pushing gently within me.

His hands in my hair, his lips at me ear, "Are you all right?"

I nodded, looking into his eyes. The pupils were wide and dark, consuming all the blue. His breath was sweet, drifting over my body as he looked down at me. The sheen on his skin, the sweat that glistened, made me want to slide my tongue over his entire body and feel him inside of me. My body shivered, doing things I didn't know it could do, wanting things I thought I'd never want. And with Jack, I wanted every bit of it.

Jack moved slowly, like I was made of glass, but that wasn't what I wanted. It felt like divine torture, as he slid in slowly, gently—barely pushing—careful not to hurt me. My mind was reeling, my skin slick and on fire. Every inch of my body wanted him. It was so carnal and raw that I screamed out, slicing his back with my nails as I pulled his chest tighter to mine.

Breathless, I said, "Take me, Jack." My voice was firm, needing him—wanting him to move in me the way my body craved. I wanted to feel the force of his thrusts inside of me. I wanted him to push into me so hard that there was only Jack, and the two of us were one. His hands held my hips, his gentle thrusts inside of me stopping as I spoke. His eyes were like blue flames, flickering with heat I didn't know he possessed. Desire glowed within their depths and only one thing would sate him, me. My words shattered him, stripping away any semblance of control he once had.

Jack, the man who was always in control, suddenly wasn't. He moved faster, pushing into me harder and harder. Our bodies moved as one, sliding and thrusting, taking us higher and higher. My mind was blank, light, and free. There was only scent and skin, slick with need. The way he moved inside of me, the position of his hands on my skin, his breath in my ear as he pushed into me—it was ecstasy filling me in the form of Jack Gray.

"Come for me Abby," he breathed in my ear. His smooth body moving against mine, his sweat filled my head, making me needy, making me spread my legs wider so he could push deeper. My body reacted to his movements, clutching against him as I came. Jack pushed into me twice more, slow and hard. He tensed, as I pulsated around him, drawing him into me. When his body relaxed, he fell onto me, kissing my face.

Covered in sweat, paint, and each other, I laid next to him feeling completely wonderful. His fingers threaded through mine, his lips pressing against the side of my face, in my hair and my lips. "Abby, oh my God." Worry creased a line between his brows. He pushed himself up and looked down at me concerned, "Did I hurt you? I shouldn't have done that to you. It was too much too fast." He was shaking his head, but I put my hand on his cheek and he stilled, his face still full of worry.

"I'm fine," I smiled. Every bit of my body felt like it was glowing softly, humming. "Jack, that was perfect. More than I thought it'd be."

He grinned, sliding down on his side so he could look at me. "More than you thought? How long have you been thinking these kinds of things, Abby?"

I didn't think it was possible, but I felt the blush rise to my face. Turning away, grinning, I started to roll over, but Jack pulled me back, locking me on the floor beneath him, pinning me with his arm. "From the look on your face, I would think quite a bit longer than would be considered, um, what's the word I'm looking for...?" his voice trailed off as his smile deepened, leaning his head to mine, he said, "oh, yeah—prudent." He pressed a kiss to my forehead and pulled away a little, enough to see my full lips smiling sheepishly.

Smiling, completely sated, I said, "It's not like I meant to. Sometimes thoughts would enter my mind. I chased them away with a Biblical broom, but they kept coming back when I wasn't able to stop them."

His dark brow arched, a crooked grin on his face in disbelief, "You dreamed about me?"

Squirming, I replied, "Sometimes, yes. The memory of you—of us—would light up in my mind making me rather hot and bothered for a preacher." I smiled at him, loving every moment of this. When his face turned serious my stomach clenched. I wanted him happy, elated and carefree.

"Abby," he twirled one of my long reddish curls that was laying over my shoulder and on my breast, gliding his fingers along the sensitive skin. Something was bothering him, but my nakedness was distracting, pulling him away from the thoughts that made him serious, but he couldn't shake it. He didn't drop the thought and soon I understood why. "I tried to keep this from happening, because I didn't want to make you miserable. This doesn't jive with what you believe at all, does it? I mean, doing erotic things and having sex on the floor... it's not a marriage bed."

I understood what he meant, "Jack, don't worry. This wasn't wrong in my head." He looked at me, shocked, his perfect lips hanging open. I pressed a finger to his mouth, closing it, smiling softly at him. "I'm not the evangelical nut you seem to think I am. It's not like that. There are a lot of things that don't jive, and I just try to make the best of them. Like you. I feel funny saying this to you, since it's about you and you can tell how long I've been enamored by you, but I will. It's the only way you'll see that I'm all right."

His fingers pressed into my hair, his palm cupping my cheek, hanging on my every word. "Please tell me, Abby. Because right now I'm thinking that as soon as the lust clears you're going to hate me." His gaze remained on mine. That haunted fear depicted in his paintings was lingering in their depths.

"Don't worry, Jack. This fits with what I believe, and it wasn't made up on the fly. A long time ago I decided that soulmates were the best part of Creation. It's a rare blessing to find someone who you can understand on a deeper level, but a soulmate goes beyond that. It's like the two are linked, as if they were made for each other, like Eve was made for Adam. She not only shared his flesh, his body, but she shared his soul. There's nothing closer than that. Marriage wasn't even on the table then, and they were together. There are lots of other stories, haunting and horrible, where God's people found their soulmate only to discover that they couldn't be together. Others broke propriety and slept together before they were married. Ruth would be a total slut by today's standards. She was a poor woman, and slept with her master because her mother-in-law told her to. But that wasn't the only reason. She loved him. They were made for each other..." my voice drifted off, realizing that I'd just told him much more than I thought I would. It wasn't that I wanted to hide it from him, it was that I was afraid of his reaction. The concept of a soulmate was so much more binding than the concept of marriage. It was more than monogamy. It was not having eyes for anyone else. It was being so lost in your lover that you weren't complete without them.

"You think we're soulmates?" he asked softly, taking a deep breath. I nodded. Understanding crossed his face. "That's why... That's why you said you'd already fallen." He shook his head, seemingly annoyed with himself.

My heart fluttered with worry. Pushing up on my elbows, I looked over at him. "I teased you in high school because you had this try-it-before-you-buy-it mentality with women, so I thought that it wasn't you—that you weren't made for me. That moment of insanity, that second where I tried to kiss you so long ago," I took a deep breathe, "that was what my gut was telling me, that you were made for me and I you. There's no reason why you have to accept it at all, Jack. You asked, you wanted to make sure I'm okay, and I am." Nervousness filled my stomach like cold eels. I wanted to squirm, run away, and hide—but I forced myself to sit there and wait for his blue eyes to narrow on me. I had to wait for his smooth lips to move and accept or reject me.

His hand fell away from my face while I was talking, his gaze falling on the canvas below us. When I'd finished there was silence. Jack stared, unblinking for way too long. My heart felt like it was going to explode, but he finally answered, "You're gut wasn't wrong, Abby. I wasn't the player you thought I was. I'd done stuff, yeah, but not everything. And not with everyone I dated. There was something missing with them. Something I did have with you. I guarded what we had, I was so afraid of it slipping away, that I didn't see what was in front of me."

Heart pounding in my ears, I replied, "What was that, Jack?"

His lips pulled up into a perfectly crooked grin, "Abby, there's always been something missing when you're not around. I never connected with anyone the way I do with you, and I never wanted anyone as much as I wanted you." His blue gaze pierced through my haze of shock. He still seemed hesitant, withdrawn. A confession was on his lips. I held back, wanting to both throw my arms around him and wanting to run. The look in his eyes made me cringe. "But I've made mistakes, Abby. There have been others. I'm not pure like you."

I already knew that. Relief washed through me. "Jack, you didn't know. Neither did I. The past is the past. We found each other. That's all that matters." While I was speaking, I moved to my knees, and kneeled in front of him taking his face in my hands, feeling his stubble against my palms. "I love you, Jack." I pressed a gentle kiss against his lips, but he pulled me against his bare chest, kissing me harder.

When he came up for air, he was smiling wide, "You keep saying all the good things first!" he teased. "I was going to say that. I was going to tell you that I loved you, that I loved you from the first moment I saw you, and want to love you for the rest of my life. Life without you, Abby, you've seen what it was—the paintings—you saw me in them, how lonely and unhappy I was..." his voice trailed off. He swallowed hard, his lashes lowering as he looked down at me, kneeling naked before him, "I'm never letting you go, Abby Tyndale."

CHAPTER TWENTY-TWO

The rest of the night passed in bliss and we slept until the sun was high in the sky. Jack was certain of us, of me, that he didn't push some angelic creature off a cliff. The more he thought about it, the more he liked the idea that I was his—body, mind and soul. We were eating take-out from the Chinese place later. I pushed around a dumpling, trying to grab it with chopsticks and failing while Jack was saying, "You're amazing." His tone had taken that bedroom voice of his again.

"Ah, yes. My ability to repel dumplings with a stick is quite a feat. Wait until you see me with seafood. Julia Roberts has nothing on me, well, in terms of shell fish shooting off my plate. I'm guessing her hooker character was better in bed." I grinned at him, and finally just stabbed the dumpling with one of the chopsticks. I lifted it to my lips, but stopped when I saw Jack staring. "What?" The food hovered, as I looked at him quizzically.

"I would have never thought you were a virgin," he blurted out.

The dumpling slid off my stick and bounced across the table. We both watched it slide into a white carton before resuming eye contact. "What?" I asked, shocked he'd say such a thing.

"Okay, so now wasn't the best time to bring it up, but you were the one talking about hookers and slamming yourself. Abby, you're the best I've ever been with."

I laughed, pointing the empty chopstick at him, "Uh huh." I didn't believe him. Actually, I believed he was trying to spare me my feelings. "Tell me why that is?"

Jack leaned across the table, taking my hands, pulling me toward him. When I gazed up at him, he said, "Because you don't hold back. You said what you meant, and moved how you felt. You have no idea how sexy that is, how much power that gives you over me. Abby, I nearly came watching you strip. When you added the paint I was frozen. The last thing I wanted to say was no. If that's what you do when you're a virgin, I can't wait to see what you do later." He grinned wickedly at me, squeezing my hand once and releasing it. Eyeing me from his seat he added, "And I know you're sore. I promise I won't touch you for the rest of the day." I squirmed, wondering how he could tell. He glanced up at me, "Well, I won't touch you there. It doesn't mean we can't have fun doing other things."

My breath caught in my throat. Suddenly I wasn't very hungry. Staring at him, I asked, "What other things?"

"Your curiosity is dangerous, Tyndale," he replied grinning.

Tilting my head, "Your evasion was noted, Gray."

"Eat your food, Abby. You're going to need your strength." He winked at me and I flushed. Heart pounding in my chest, I felt my sore girl parts perk up—ready for more Jack Gray.

CHAPTER TWENTY-THREE

The canvas from the sex painting was still wet. Jack hung it on the wall, letting it dry. Hands on his hips, he stepped back admiring it. My stomach fluttered a little when I looked at it. Okay, it fluttered a lot and made me tingle in all my girlie places. It was hot. To everyone else it looked like one of Jack's works gone more abstract, but to us, it meant something else.

It was a beginning.

Perched on a tabletop, I sat swinging my legs and staring at Jack's ass. I didn't realize I was doing it until he glanced over his shoulder to ask me a question. His arms were folded against his chest as his eyes shifted, full of mischief and lust—like mine. My lips pursed when he saw me. I was going to deny it, but shrugged instead, and said "You're easy on the eyes, Gray. What do you want me to say?"

"Did you always ogle me so openly and I never noticed?"

I laughed, hanging my head, my hair falling forward. I flipped my hair back as he walked over to me, a sexy grin on his face. "At times. It's hard not to admire you when you're standing so perfectly." That thought brought a question to the front of my mind. "Is that what you meant by saying I was all shapes and lines? Shadows and light? Was that to conceal your lusting eyes from me?"

He laughed, "They weren't concealed, and if you knew what I was thinking that night, you wouldn't have come back."

"Why's that? What hideously kinky thoughts were you thinking?" His words peaked my curiosity. I slid off the table and stepped in front of him, looking into his eyes, knowing there were only a few days of this left. Only a handful of days before everyone was back at the studio.

He sighed a ragged breath, running his fingers through his hair. Damn, he was hot. Every mannerism he had made me want him more. My tongue touched my top lip as I watched him. "Abby," he groaned, throaty and raw—the same way he said my name last night. "You're killing me."

I hadn't realized what I'd done until Jack seemed to melt in front of me. He grinned, his eyes dark and needy as they slid over me. Slipping his hands around my waist, he yanked me up against him. I could feel him stiff and ready. I gasped, "Jack." He pushed me away, as if teasing me, tempting me.

Shaking his head, he said smiling, dimples showing, "We're going to have to make up for missing ten years of sex in a couple of days, aren't we?" I blushed, looking up at him through lowered lashes, but I very much liked the sound of that. "Damn, Abby. I'm the luckiest man alive. Ten years of sex in two days." His body tensed as his gaze slid over me, lingering on my breasts, noticing my nipples showing through my tee shirt. The bottom of my stomach fell when he looked at me like that. I was sure I was wet again.

I nodded, "Sounds fine by me."

He whispered in my ear, his hand sliding over the curve of my breast while he spoke, "It'll be better than fine. You'll be so sated, so wonderfully satisfied that you'll be sore for a week."

"Then do it, painter boy. Show me what you want, what you like." I tilted my head to the side, hair falling away from my face. "Jack, what are we waiting for? If I'm going to be sore anyway, why wait?" I was seriously asking. I didn't know much about this. I'd always tried to tame my sexuality, and subdue the urges of the flesh. And right then, my urges wanted our flesh naked, sliding together.

Taking me by the face, Jack thrust his fingers into my hair, tugging gently as I spoke. His eyes grew darker as his breathing slowed, becoming deeper. "You undo me, Abby. I'm completely lost, and want to give you anything and everything you ask for, but there's one thing I want."

My lips were close to his, "What's that?"

"I want to take you, be with you without worrying that I'm hurting you." He ran his fingers through my hair, his hot hands sliding against my cheek.

"Didn't you do that already? Last night?"

He nodded, "That's part of the reason you were sore. It was too soon." Disappointment must have been visible on my face. Kissing my lips softly, he said, "There are other ways to be together. Other things to do that are just as sexy. Abby, let me give you today my way. Let me show you other things, things you may like just as much as feeling me inside of you." The heat that pumped into me as he spoke made me lose my ability to speak. I nodded, agreeing to his proposal.

He smiled, "Promise me one thing, though. No matter what we do today, no matter how hot you get, don't ask me to fuck you because I won't be able to tell you no." Biting my lower lip, eyes locked on his—mesmerized—I nodded.

CHAPTER TWENTY-FOUR

Jack was on a ladder, unstrapping his camera from the ceiling. I was going to be the object of his adoration in a photo shoot. The idea made me nervous and excited at the same time. To distract myself from the butterflies swarming in my stomach, I asked, "What are you doing about your business leak?"

Not turning to look down, he continued to untwist the screws that clamped the camera in place. "Well, I've discovered that I'm completely in love with the main suspect, and that there's no way in hell she did it. However, I can't use the deductive reasoning I used with her on everyone else."

I snorted, "I should hope not. Gus would file a sexual harassment claim in a heartbeat." He laughed, shaking his head.

"Gus is a partner, he'd be filing the claim against himself if he did that."

My lip curled, "Yuck. Let's not talk about what Gus does to himself." I was joking, and it was way more raunchy than the things I usually said. Where the hell did that come from?

Jack snorted, nearly dropping the camera, "What's gotten into you? You go from being a nun to a..."

"To a what, Jack?" I grinned, coaxing him on.

"To a seductress, Abby. To a foul-mouthed seductress with a dirty mind." He shook his head, smiling hard, "I'm so lucky."

Getting back on track, I asked, "Well, what about it? How'd Belinda get your contact list?"

"I don't know yet. There's no paper trail. I went through emails, notes, and tons of stuff—there's nothing. No outbound calls to her number either. I haven't found anything, Abby, which is a problem. It means she either hacked in, or the person that's helping her is so far beyond reproach that I'd never suspect them. In the meantime, it breaks apart the studio, and alienates my staff as I lose each and every one of you. Who's going to stick around after being accused of something like that?"

Feeling impish, I offered, "I did." He glanced down at me, stopping what he was doing.

"You're different. You're not like them; you're not like anyone else I've ever met, Abby. You think with your heart, no matter the cost." He stared at me for a moment, his eyes locking onto mine. I'd always thought of that as a flaw, one-hundred percent effective way to die as a martyr, but Jack looked at me like it was something valuable—something to be admired. He broke the gaze, smiling faintly before pulling the camera down in his hands. Slowly, he crept down the ladder, one rung at a time with a costly piece of equipment in one hand, the other making sure he didn't drop twenty feet to the floor. Jumping off the bottom step like a little boy, he sauntered toward me, camera in one hand, and a sexy grin on his face. "I want to show you what I see when I look at you. It's not the girl you see in the mirror, and I can tell that you don't really know what I mean. Do you trust me Abby? Will you pose for me? Wear what I ask? Do what I ask?"

If he said, *Would you do striptease for me, here's a boa,* I would have laughed and hit him in the chest. But this request was so sexually charged. It felt like he was devouring me with his eyes. That gaze crushed the air out of my lungs, rendering me unable to speak. Deep within my body, things clenched in that delicious way that made me feel like his seductress. I nodded, "I'll try," I whispered.

A stern look shadowed his face, "No, there's not trying. You either will or you won't." His eyes gleamed, locking onto mine with an intense need. It made me nod without thinking. I didn't know what he liked, and I sure as hell wanted to know what he saw when he looked at me. Was that something that he could capture with a lens? I didn't know. "Say it," he whispered, firmly telling me to speak.

"Yes. I'll do it. I want to see what you see." My eyes drifted from his perfect lips to his intense eyes. I breathed, "I trust you, Jack." My heart was racing in my chest as his expression softened. The man that was looking at me a moment ago was part of the Jack that I didn't know—the one who'd been burned. He didn't mess around, he wanted direct, firm, decisions, and nothing less. When he turned away, he placed the camera on a table top and said he'd be right back.

Moving toward the large black square, I lifted the camera off the table. Fumbling with the buttons, I wondered if the photos from the shoot with my first painting were still on it. I found the right buttons, and clicked them hoping to see something from that night. The canvas was covered on the wall. Jack concealed it, telling me he wanted me to wait until he was done to see it. Looking at the camera was totally cheating. A small thrill coursed through me as I clicked the button, expecting to see the fluffy skirt and my naked chest covered in paint, but the screen was black. I frowned.

Jack whispered behind me, making me jump, "I took the card out—and you're a horrible snoop. You aren't supposed to get caught." He gave me a look that made me smile sheepishly as he ripped the camera out of my hands. "It'll be the best painting I've ever made. Give it time, Abby. Let me finish it." He smiled, his expression warming. I didn't understand why he was being secretive, why I was denied seeing the process, but I didn't press him.

Jack had placed the camera on the table behind him. There were several thin boxes that he had brought back when he snuck up on me. I reached for the lid, but Jack swatted my fingers away. "Not yet," he laughed. "Go change. I hung up the skirt you wore—the one I painted—it's in the dressing room. Put that on and come out."

"Just the skirt?" I asked, suddenly feeling shy. Jack's eyes pierced me, raking across my body, landing on my face and finally meeting my gaze.

"Just the skirt." Stubble lined his jaw, making his eyes appear brighter, bluer. Air rushed out of my lungs in a shallow gasp. For some reason, doing this in the middle of the day seemed more risqué than doing it in the middle of the night. But the look in his eye told me the skirt was only the beginning.

I came out of the dressing room, my arm covering my chest, as I held up the huge skirt with my other hand, walking toward him. Jack stood next to three open boxes of glittering jewels. When I was close enough to see what they were, my jaw dropped. "Jack, are those real?" Of course they were real. He was rich, but I never seemed to remember that. I saw my high school version of Jack, the boy clad in jeans and Chuck's. The man worth millions was watching me, grinning at the arm covering my body.

His dark brow arched as he stepped toward me, "As real as you are, but your perfection makes them seem trite." He reached for my hands, forcing me to reveal myself. The muscles in my arms were tense. There were no midnight hour, sleepy, half-conscious minds making decisions. This time was different. This time I was giving myself to him in way that I hadn't done before. I knew he wanted me, but I didn't know how, and the look in his eyes said it would be different. He held me at arm's length, my hands in his as he parted them, holding my arms away from my body, admiring me. Jack's hot gaze slipped over my neck, lingered on my breasts, before dipping to my waist. He released one hand and raised the other. "Spin," he commanded, passing me under his arm. I spun once slowly, on the ball of my foot feeling like a wanton ballerina, wishing that he'd touch me—but Jack only watched.

His eyes slid over me as I turned, caressing the curves of my body, seeing them in the full light from the window. My heart pounded in my chest. I glanced at the open window, worried. He saw my gaze pass his shoulder and land on the glass. "No one's here, Abby. It's private property. Trust me." My eyes moved back to his face. I nodded once, and didn't look at the window again.

Jack took a deep breath, smiling to himself. "You are so stunning, so captivatingly beautiful." He breathed heavily, his eyes growing darker. He blinked once. Twice. Forcing away the emotions that were dominating him. "I'm going to reposition this," he took a fist full of skirt, tugging it, "and then the jewelry." I nodded, still feeling exposed, still shocked by how much I wanted him.

Barefoot, I padded behind him to a table filled with brushes, tiny tubes, palettes, and shears. Jack picked up a silver pair of scissors. He gripped my waist, and tugged at the skirt until the slit was in front—off center—over my leg. He pushed the fabric back, seeing my lack of panties, and smiled. Leaning closer, he kneeled in front of me, pressing his face to my bare skin and inhaled. My fingers found his hair and as I tried to hold him there, but Jack pulled away, his hair getting tugged as he retreated.

Every inch of me was tingling, aching to be touched. Without thinking, I whispered, "You're making me crazy, Jack." I breathed deeply, my chest expanding fully as he looked up at me.

"Remember, your promise, Abby." With that he took the skirt in his hands, and layer by layer hacked into it. When he was done, it looked like a wild animal had eaten the front of the skirt. There wasn't any fabric left to cover anything below the waist. The remnants of the skirt trailed down behind my waist, covering my butt. I swallowed hard, trying to remain still and silent.

Jack stepped back, his fingers touching his face, arms folded, as he surveyed the new slutty skirt. Hesitating for a moment, he seemed to come to a conclusion. Practically running, Jack bounced over to the storage racks and climbed up. He dug a black piece of satin from one, and a pair of shiny black heels from another. "Size 7?" he asked, before jumping down. I nodded, frozen. This felt erotic, making me feel vulnerable in a good way.

Jack walked back toward me. It seemed like he deliberately slowed his step. I commented on it, "Less eager now, are we?" My voice had bravado that I didn't feel. I wondered where it came from, as he walked toward me holding heels that had to be a health hazard. They promised broken ankles and other naughty things that made my cheeks burn.

Jack stopped in his tracks when the rosy glow spread across my body. His eyes slid over me, his hands gripping the shoes tighter, and crushing the scrap of black fabric. He breathed deeply, his chest rising, his eyes focused. "Every time you say something, I have the insatiable urge to sink my fingers into your ass and take you." My blush deepened as I looked down, trying to hide it. Jack continued to walk toward me, slowly, seductively. My heart beat faster with every step. He looked like he wanted to do those things and more. "Eagerness does not begin to describe what I want to do with you." He held out the shoes. I reached and took them.

They were black patent. The toe was so pointed, I didn't know if they'd fit. The heel was at least four inches. I usually wore ballet flats or sandals. I slipped one on, trying to stand, looking at the other sexy shoe in my hand, "Jack, I don't know if I can walk in these."

He grinned, "They're not for walking, Abby." I blushed harder. "There's a reason they're called fuck-me heels. They're recreational shoes." I knew what they were called. I was a minister; I didn't live in a bubble. I just never owned a pair. There was no reason to, but with the way Jack watched me, I wished I had. I slipped on the second shoe and was lucky I could stand up. My ankles were threatening to wobble, when Jack's gaze slid over my body, appreciatively. His arms folded across his chest, the curve of his pecs outlined perfectly.

I felt such a strange mixture of things as he looked at me, lust and sensuality climbed to the top, crushing the shyness that was dormant beneath. Oh,

I wanted him to touch me. I wanted his hands on my body, feeling my curves and not just tracing them with his eyes. Jack crooked a finger at me. "Come here."

I took a step in the shoes, carefully moving toward him. His eyes locked on my body, my breasts thrust forward, the angle of my butt forced out from the insanely high shoes. I stopped in front of him, willing him to touch me. He lifted his hand, pressing a single finger to my neck. His skin was warm, barely touching me as he trailed his hand down the curve of my neck, caressing the soft flesh of my breast, and causing me to gasp when he lightly brushed my taut nipple. I glanced up at him in wonder. He made me feel so much, and I wanted more.

"Jack," I moaned, ready to beg him, but he stopped me.

Smiling softly, eyes full of lust, he said, "Your promise, Abby. Seal those sexy lips before I give you something to suck on." The seductive threat made a pool of heat shoot straight to my core. His words only made me want him more. The idea of tasting him was beyond appealing, and once he mentioned it, I couldn't clear the thought from my mind. "Abby. You're so incredibly hot. The fact that you're like this and have only been with me makes it hotter." His gaze rested on my face for a moment. It was like we were both lost all these years and we'd finally found each other. He stepped toward me, gently running his fingers down the side of my face, making my heart pound harder. My eyes closed as he spoke, "You're mine." Opening my eyes, I nodded. There was something in his expression, something hotter, more dark and desperate than he seemed a moment ago. "Last chance to back out."

I shook my head slowly, "I'm not going anywhere. It's everything I can do to keep from begging you to touch me. If you blew on me, I swear I'd lose it." My breath hitched. Jack's hands moved under the skirt, reaching around to my bare ass, and pulled me against him. The bulge in his pants felt so hard. I wanted to feel him inside me.

"Stop talking, Miss Tyndale. Not a word for the rest of the shoot." His hands squeezed me hard, before releasing me. He looked down, smiling softly to himself, as I nodded. Silence. I could be silent, right?

Jack turned his back and lifted the jewels out of the case. It was a layered pearl necklace – each pearl perfectly round and perfectly black. I eyed the jewelry. Jack brushed my hair aside, lifting the necklace to my throat. It fastened tightly, with multiple rows of pearls hanging down. Each row dipped further and further, finally dipping down between my breasts. The rows were tightly nuzzled, showing little flesh between the perfect pearls.

"This set was made by Tiffany's—special request. I had a vision of someone wearing it several years ago," he glanced to the side as he touched the pearls, making me gasp. "A dream, I guess. A beautiful redhead, the girl that haunts me was sitting at my feet draped in black pearls, half naked." I started to open my mouth to say something, but he pressed his fingers to my lips. "I swear to God, Abby, if you say another thing I'll tease you for the next two days and not let you come once." My shoulders stiffened. That sounded wonderful and horrible at the same time.

He grinned. "Come here," I stepped toward him. He slipped his hand between my legs, pushing them up, feeling how wet I was. Withdrawing his hand, he locked his eyes with mine. Putting each finger in his mouth, one at a time, he licked me off his fingers. My body was already in overdrive. His fingers touching me made me feel more, want more, but watching him do that—I couldn't hide how much I liked it. Before I could gasp or anything else, he reached for more jewelry. Another rope of pearls was draped around my waist, and twisting waterfall earrings of a million tiny pearls and diamonds sparkled in my ears. He grazed my breasts, putting them on me, but I remained still and silent, proud of myself. The last piece he pulled from the box was a triple row of tiny pearls strung across a silver chain. I looked at him, wondering where that would go. I was already covered head to toe in pearls.

Jack held the two ends up, showing me a tiny hook. "These are breast jewelry, Abby. They dangle from your nipples." My jaw dropped slightly. I didn't see how they attached. Jack saw the question in my eyes. He grabbed me by the waist as I started to step away, stopping me, the rows of pearls sliding beneath his palms. "This is the last piece. The hook is padded with plastic. It slides over your nipples, and clamps on. It'll feel like me pinching you. It'll hurt a little, but in a good way."

I froze, watching his hands move toward me. Part of me was ecstatic, the other part hesitant, but Jack's hands were on me, pulling my tender flesh softly, teasing me firmer between his fingers melting any remaining reluctance. I gasped, unable to contain myself. At the same time the rush of air came out of my lungs, he fastened one side onto my breast. It pinched tightly, pulling me gently. Jack's hand started working the other side. Within moments, both hooks were pinched over my sensitive breasts, pulling the nipples with the weight of the chains and pearls.

Jack watched me, darkness glinting in his eyes, hungry. He moved across the room, pulling down a black backdrop from a roll of canvases on one side of the studio. His voice made warmth pool between my legs. "Come." He pointed to the backdrop.

As I crossed the room, he closed the window shades, sealing out the light. My ankles protested with each step I took in the heels. The beads shook while I walked, the breast jewelry making me moan, shooting hot sparks through all the right places. Jack's eyes watched me move through the darkness, his hands folded over his chest. He didn't offer to help, he just gazed, unblinking—his blue eyes dark as sapphires, hot as coals.

I stopped in front of him, standing on the canvas, nearly climaxing from my short walk. Reaching for the nipple chain, he tugged lightly, and breathed, "Not yet, preacher-girl." I gasped, a rush of air ripping from my throat. The sensations that flooded my body when he pulled the chain and made me tremble.

Jack smiled, enjoying every moment of my exotic agony. "If you're a very good girl, if you do everything I ask, I'll make sure you feel completely satisfied at the end of the shoot." My mind felt so drugged with lust that I barely caught what he said. The moment after it registered, I glanced at him. He was holding his camera up. "Deal?" I nodded. Hell yes. I would have done anything at that point. Reason was forced out, and only desire for Jack remained.

The poses were sexy at first, mainly because of my outfit—if you could call it that—which I wasn't sure I could. Being draped in pearls, diamonds, and silver with a skirt that didn't cover anything wasn't the kind of wardrobe I would have called an outfit. But Jack's dark gaze, the want in his eyes as he posed me, as he shot me, made me feel like the sexiest woman he'd ever seen. The first poses I stood with my ankles apart, showing the long lines of my naked legs, facing the camera, hands over my head showcasing the jewelry adorning my body like I was Cinderella going to the exhibitionist's ball. The shutter snapped again and again. Jack repositioned the poses, moved the lighting. They flashed every time he shot, making me feel more glamorous.

I tried to squeeze my thighs together to help ease the lust that was building beyond control within me. Gravity was pulling on the chains on my breasts, so that even when I didn't move, the sensations didn't stop. Jack's face was hidden behind his camera, concealing his thoughts. Finally, when my knees were pressed so tightly together that my legs were shaking, he said, "Sit, legs apart, arms in front of you like this," he held out his hands, one wrist touching the other. Slowly, I sank to the floor, closing my eyes, feeling the exquisite sensation tugging on me. My legs were together off to the side. When I pulled them apart, I went to copy the pose of his arms, but Jack stopped me. Walking over to me, he kept my legs curled to the side, but separated my ankles. "Like that," he said when he was done, "Now reach for me Abby." I lifted my arms toward his face, but he smiled, saying, "Reach for me, Abby. Like you want me, like you want to taste me." My breath caught. My breasts were swollen, wanting his touch, sensitive. When he said those words I froze, staring at his dark jeans, wondering what it would be like. My private parts tingled thinking about it. Jack's voice was firm, "Reach for me, Abby. Reach for me before I tug that chain and make you cry out."

Swallowing hard, I reached for him. He stood close enough that my hands slid over his jeans, feeling the hard length hidden, contained under the fabric. Groaning, he said, "Good. Stay." And stepped away. I felt like I was intoxicated with Jack, and yet I still wanted more. I remained still, feeling the pull on my breasts as the sting built in my arms. He moved the lights, repositioned the back of the skirt and shot. The shutter clicked, snapping shut closer and closer to the end of the shoot.

"One more pose." I looked at him with desperation in my eyes. I wanted him so badly. The soreness I'd felt earlier was gone and nothing but my word was keeping me from attacking Jack, peeling off his clothes, and climbing on top of him.

Jack saw the passion in my eyes, as the lusty thoughts I didn't bother to conceal played across my face. He smiled, saying, "Kneel. Knees apart." I scooted in front of him, getting up on my knees, spreading my thighs. The cold air met my wet warmth and made me shiver.

Jack watched me, his lips full and open. He pressed his eyes closed, snapping himself out of the seductive trance we both fell into and moved behind me. He fanned the crinoline skirt so that it billowed from my waist, pooling behind me like a sea of ink. He leaned over, standing in front of me, meeting my gaze. "Last set, okay? As soon as I have it, you're going to come fast and hard—and not make a sound." His lips twisted into a smile. I couldn't take my eyes off of them as he pulled away from my face.

"Hands over your head, Tyndale." I draped both hands on top of my head, thinking that was what he wanted, but it wasn't. "Almost done. Now, take one hand and stretch, reach as high as you can. Thrust your chest toward the light, and close your eyes."

I closed my eyes, and did as he said. Stretching as far as I could with one hand, I reached over my head. It made my body curve and forced my breasts toward him, the silver chain swaying between them as I bent my spine back. My long hair tickled my bare back. The shutter snapped several times, moving around me. I didn't move. I could hear Jack breathing. My legs were trembling, wanting him, needing him to sate the lust that was beyond agony. Every inch of my skin burned, longing to be touched.

Without a word, Jack was behind me, on his knees whispering in my ear, "Come for me Abby." One hand moved between my legs, sliding in the damp heat. The other reached around and yanked gently on the chain strung across my breasts. The intense feelings spread through me fast. The shutter clicked once, then twice. Jack rigged the camera to keep shooting. I didn't know where it was, but the thought of Jack having pictures of me coming in his arms pushed me over the edge.

I screamed his name, "Jack," as I thrust against his hand, finding my release in his arms. Sinking back into him, I laid there, my back to his front for a moment, breathing heavily.

His hands slid around my middle, under the rows of pearls, feeling my soft flesh beneath his hands. "That was so sexy, but we're not done yet." He turned me around, his fingers squeezing my tender nipples, "We need to take these off." As he squeezed, he loosened the clamp. I closed my eyes and soon felt his lips coaxing, sucking me hard. I gasped. It almost felt like he nipped me. Jack continued to massage the hard flesh with his tongue, becoming gentler and gentler until he lifted his head and said, "Now for the other." He did the same thing, repeating every step, making me a hot mess, laying in his arms, arching my back, begging for more.

With the nipple clamps gone, he slowly removed the jewelry, laying it next to us on the floor. The last thing he did was untie the skirt and push it back. He laid back on the floor, pulling the fluffy skirt under his head like a pillow. "Come here, Abby. I want to kiss you."

I leaned down, about to press my lips to his, when he grabbed my hips, sinking his strong hands into my skin. "Not like that. Spread your legs, kneel over me." He pulled me to him, and I was half delighted, half horrified. The delighted part of my mind won the logic debate hands down. The sensible girl that usually called all the shots was promptly ignored and before I knew it, my legs were parted over his face as I straddled his head.

Jack's breath assaulted me, making it hard not to move, but he'd asked me to be still. "Abby, you smell good enough to eat." His voice was deep, husky. I started to answer but lost the ability to speak when I felt his mouth start to kiss me. It was gentle, each caress soft and strong, taking me right back to the intoxicated Jack-high I was on before. His mouth moved magically against me. Without realizing it, my hands were over my head, as Jack licked every drop of me from my sensitive skin. I was trying hard to stay still. I didn't want to hurt Jack, but the sensations that were building within me wanted to sway my hips above his lips, and press down hard.

As if he could read my mind, Jack breathed, "Ride me Abby. Move how you want. You won't hurt me." He words were the freedom I wanted. His tongue teased me into a frenzy. My body slid over his kisses, the slick warmth of his tongue making me cry out again. As I froze, feeling the perfect pulsating sensations within me, he thrust his tongue inside me, drinking me in. I gasped, surprised.

When he rolled me onto my back, I saw the lust still gleaming his eyes, "You make me want you in every possible way. I've never wanted to do that so much in my life. Every inch of you is divine, like you were sculpted for me, and me alone." He brushed the hair out of my face, kissing my face gently.

In my post-coital glow, I leaned into him saying, "This feels like a dream, and I'm afraid I'm going to wake up." My heart was slowing, beating in time with his. I could feel it beating as if we were the same person, as if he were my other half.

CHAPTER TWENTY-FIVE

Jack joined me in the shower, kissing my neck sweetly before vacating the space and leaving me alone to my thoughts. Things were so different than I thought they'd be, and it was wonderful. As the water poured over my body, I felt like I was happily floating along like a little fluffy cloud. I took time getting dressed, wanting to look as beautiful as Jack made me feel. A little over an hour passed by the time I was ready.

When I stepped into the studio, Jack's eyes wandered over my body like he still hadn't had enough. A blush rose to my cheeks. I had no idea how it was possible to do the things we did, and then blush about it later. It was like my blusher was broken or something.

Jack pulled me into his arms, his forehead touching mine, "What on earth could you be thinking to redden your beautiful face so much?" He grinned at me in a way that made my heart flutter.

Taking a deep breath, I smiled, teasingly pushing him away, "Everything you do makes me blush—no specific memory is needed."

He pulled me back into his arms, his fingers tickling my waist gently, his lips a breath from mine, "We should really go into town before I peel this dress off of you." Jack pressed his lips to my ear, gently kissing me, before pulling away.

Nodding, I said, "Just let me grab my purse."

As I opened the desk drawer, Jack said, "Grab your check, too. It's in the top drawer."

I removed my purse from the desk, and found my check. It felt kind of weird, spending the day with our naked bodies intertwined and then taking money from him. I hesitated, my hand hovering over the check. "Jack, maybe I shouldn't work here anymore."

He grabbed his keys and was pulling on a leather jacket. "Don't be silly. Why not?" I watched the narrow band of skin at his waist when he lifted his arms. He was gorgeous.

"I don't know, it just feels odd."

"Then you won't work here anymore," he smiled at me, zipping his coat. "Abby, I wanted to wait to ask you this, but I don't want you to think that you don't belong in any part of my life. What's mine is yours. What's yours is mine. The good and the bad. I want all of you. I want you forever," he knelt, taking my hand in his. My heart thumped in my ears, nearly exploding in my brain, "The last few weeks have meant everything to me. I've adored every moment we spent together and when you're away, I can't wait until you come back. It was a miracle that you walked through those doors. After all these years, I thought I'd never see you again, and the last few days have made me never want to let you go." His hands were in my hair, gently touching my curls, his blue eyes soft and perfect as he spoke. "Abby, let me spend the rest of my life loving you. Let me take care of you. Let me be a part of your life in every way possible. Abby Tyndale, will you marry me?"

My jaw dropped. What came over him? I just said something about the check. I didn't want to leave, but this—this shocked me. I'd known him forever, but we'd been apart so long. Staring at his beautiful face, I knew he was right. I felt it too. It was like we never left. Things were better than they ever had been. Despite my shocked silence, my mind was already scrawling Mrs. Abigail Gray with lots of bubbly hearts. Life with Jack was everything I ever wanted. My lips trembled as I tried not to smile, and refused to cry.

Jack rubbed the back of my hand, looking up at me, waiting. A gleeful sob bubbled over my lips as I beamed, throwing my arms around his neck, kissing him furiously, not coming up for air even when my lungs burned. When we managed to break apart, I was shaking, crying, and laughing.

Pushing my hair out of my face, he held me in his arms, smiling so hard. "I take that as a yes?"

Nodding and wiping tears from my eyes, I said, "Yes!"

CHAPTER TWENTY-SIX

Jack wasn't kidding when he said that he planned on proposing. When we went into town, he took me to a stunning waterfront restaurant. It was crowded, but the waiter took us in, walking past many jealous eyes, all the way into the back. We passed through carved oak doors that lead to a private room that overlooked the water. And the room was totally empty.

I glanced at Jack surprised, but he only shrugged, "I wanted to be alone with you. I had an important question to ask." He grinned, taking my hand in his, holding it tighter.

My eyes were wide, "How much did you have to pay them to leave this space open? Jack!" I was smiling too much. My face hurt, the muscles felt overused, but it was a welcome soreness like I had in other parts of my body. I sucked at taking gifts graciously, but I was trying. During dinner, I could barely stay on my side of the table. His eyes moved over me like he wanted me for dinner, not the beautiful meal on his plate.

About half way through the meal, he took his phone from his pocket. Flicking the screen, he said, "Would you like to see your shoot, Mrs. Gray?"

Two things happened simultaneously. First, I flushed, hushing him like people would hear, but no one was around. Second, my smile couldn't be contained when he called me Mrs. Gray. It felt like someone squeezed my heart, making that empty space in my chest fade into oblivion. In a hushed voice, I asked, "You brought them with you? When did you even look at them?"

He grinned, "You take long showers."

A coy smile laced across my lips, "I was very dirty, Mr. Gray." He smiled harder, the little lines at the corners of his eyes crinkled. Jack was so beautiful.

The waiters stayed away, out of sight but ready to come if Jack turned his head in their direction. I squirmed a little. I didn't know how I felt about seeing the portraits, or about viewing them in public. However, I did like that Jack had them with him, hidden on his phone. It made me feel daring and free. He nodded, a tapered finger flicking the screen, the expression on his face becoming sexier by the moment. "Come over here."

I walked around the table feeling like we shouldn't be doing this, but Jack didn't seem to care. He pulled me on his lap, warm arms wrapping around me. I could feel how much he wanted me, and closed my eyes enjoying the sensation. His hand draped across my knee, before the other one produced the iPhone. "Now, let me warn you. This is the sexiest shoot I've ever seen in my entire life." Leaning closer, brushing his lips to my ear he whispered, "Are you sure you want to see?" His eyes glinted as his sexy smile widened.

"Jack," I was ready to ride him right there. The entire day passed and he sated me again and again, but he still hadn't been back inside of me where I wanted him. Fighting the urge to writhe on his lap, I pressed my knees together and said, "Show me before I wiggle on your lap so much that I leave an embarrassing little wet spot."

He flushed, "Abby!" Jack's face had the most delightful expression, part awe and part embarrassment. Trying to knock me off-kilter, he held up the phone, and the screen illuminated, showcasing me, decked out in pearls and silver. The way the light lit my body, the dark pearls and inky skirt draping off of me, the glittering chain that went from one nipple to the other—I squealed and ripped the phone out of his hands. He laughed, taking in my reaction.

Looking over both shoulders, I concealed the phone, half looking at it and half hiding it. "You can't take pictures like that, Jack!" My pink lips hung open, slightly shocked and very turned on.

He reached for the phone, trying to take it from me, a smile snaking its way across his lips. "And why not? When the model is this sexy, what'd you think the pictures would look like? Hiding you as a nun for a decade seriously threw me off, but this is what you are, Abby. This is what I see when I look at you." He laughed, still trying to get the phone.

"But, Jack, they're so dirty." I held it away from him, feeling like I'd fall off his lap, but he held me tight. I flicked the screen, trying to see another picture, fascinated and afraid. The picture was dark, nearly solid black except for a rim light surrounding my upper body. It drew attention to my breasts, both taut nipples, my lashes lowered with full lips. I didn't know who that girl was, but as I looked at her Jack glanced from the phone and back to me like he was seeing the same thing.

Tucking a piece of hair behind my ear he said, "Look at the next one," I flicked the screen. The next picture was more sensual, more erotic and more beautiful. I gasped, not believing what I was seeing. I was there; I was at the shoot, but I had no idea I looked like this. The pit of my stomach twisted, delighted and nervous.

Jack spoke softly in my ear, "That's what you do to me—when I see you and I can't have you—that's how you make me feel." The phone felt like a brick in my hand. The portrait was everything, his longing, my desire—unmet, like we were when I first saw him sitting across the table from me as he stole my interview from Gus. The phone slid out of my hand and hit the floor. Our bodies inched together, my lips burning, wanting to feel his mouth against mine. We leaned in toward each other, lost in lust when the door to the galley swung open. I glanced down, heat rising to my cheeks. Standing, I slid off his lap and moved back to my seat.

Without a word, the waiter went to walk away, embarrassed, but Jack said, "Check. Now." His blue eyes were locked on mine, not looking away as he said it. Those pictures made my head spin. They were the most erotic depictions I'd ever seen—and they were of me. It wasn't just that they were nudes, it was that they were evocative. Everything about them screamed of deep longing and sexuality unsurpassed.

My voice was thin, "Is that really how you see me, Jack? All the time?" my brows lifted, like I didn't believe what I was saying. My hands were on the table in front of me strangling the helpless tablecloth in my death-grip.

Jack took my hands, running his thumb along the back of my hand, tilting his head. "There wasn't a time when I didn't see you like that. You've always been that way to me, Abby—an unattainable goddess."

The room was silent, as he handed me the phone. Glancing down, I took it and flipped through more pictures, each more sensual than the last, lust building through the shoot—the way that it had been building in my body—until the final image was of the two of us together. Jack was holding me, and the expression on my face was completely sated.

My eyes glanced up and saw Jack, his gaze dark and wanting. He'd done it to me again, turned me into something I wasn't. As if he could read my thoughts he said, "I just bring it out in you, Abby. This sensuality, this exquisite sexuality has always been there. It always will be. It's part of who you are."

CHAPTER TWENTY-SEVEN

Our night was perfect. Utterly divine. We walked past the jeweler's closed shop, heads tilted together, Jack's arms around my waist. "I'll take you here tomorrow. We'll pick out the perfect ring for you."

"Jack, this feels like a dream," I snuggled in his strong arms. He pressed a kiss to my temple as we watched the lit window. Different rings, all amazing, filled the case.

Jack said, "I like that one. The one that looks vintage with the antique setting. It's stunning, just like you." And it was a stunning ring. At least five carats. I didn't know how I felt about that, about Jack's money. Even though I'd been back for a while, and seen him running his business, I still thought of him as the strapped guy that I knew in high school. He worked his ass off, like me, and neither of us ever had much. As if he sensed my thoughts, he said, "It's our money now, Abby. What's mine is yours. You won't have to think about anything ever again. And that church off. You never have to go back there again. I'm paying your loans off first thing in the morning."

I laughed softly. The idea of telling the church to go to Hell was appealing. At the rate they were going, they were headed there anyway. Part of me wanted to fight with Jack, and resist. "They didn't do it—they didn't sign for the loans. I did. Those were my mistakes, Jack. I thought I could do it. I thought I could find a balance between idealism and reality, but there wasn't one. I made all the wrong choices."

Turning me in his arms so that I faced him, Jack took my chin in one hand, leaving his other on my waist, "Look at me, Abby. You made all the right choices. Everything you did brought us back together. Those decisions gave us a chance that we wouldn't have had. I'd love you to tell them to screw off, that you don't need them anymore. What that church did to you was..." he bit his lip, shaking his head. He softened his tone and continued, "They trapped you. They figured out a way to keep you indebted to them and trapped you. When you sold all their crap and gave the money to the poor, you blindsided them. They were a means, a way to bring you back to me. I can't stand what they did to you, but there's no way I'd wish it didn't happen, because without them, you wouldn't be here with me now." I breathed deeply, trying to let go of the emotions tied to that place.

Tears formed in my eyes, "If it was a good thing, then why do I feel like I failed? I didn't save anyone. Seminary, all that debt, the last decade of my life—it was for nothing."

Smiling softly, he pressed his lips to my forehead. Wiping away my tears, he said, "You saved me. Abby, I was so lost before you came back. Life was a never ending series of fake people hoping to get a piece of me. No one actually sees me as person. I'm a fucking bag of money, a means to an ends. The models do it, the business partners do it, the patrons do—everyone sees me the same way. I was sick of it.

I couldn't stand it anymore. I would have dropped a match on the place and walked away. It was that bad, Abby. But the day you showed up was the day my life started again. I know misery. I know about trying to do the right thing and having it come back and bite you on the ass. And I can promise you, Abby, all that misery you went through wasn't for nothing. You told me a few weeks ago, if you saved one person, that was enough. Abby, I'm that person. You saved me."

As he spoke I watched his eyes, his lips spilling his soul. I wanted to hear the words, and silence his painful story at the same time. I could tell that there was darkness lurking within him, something dark and desperate. I saw it in him during my interview. Jack seemed cold, distant. He wasn't the boy I'd left behind all those years ago. But slowly, as days turned into weeks, I saw that boy was still inside of him. Jack began to melt, his hard edges smoothing. I didn't realize that I was the reason until that moment.

Pressing my lips to his, I kissed him softly, tears in my eyes. I held him close, in front of the shop, feeling his hair in my hands. Smiling I said, "I love you so much."

He glanced at me, grinning softly, "Come on, Mrs. Gray. There are some things I'd like to show you in my room."

CHAPTER TWENTY-EIGHT

When we walked into the studio it was pitch black, but something seemed off. My eyes shifted through the shadows trying to see what was bothering me before Jack flipped the lights on. As he did so, we could see the files in the desk were dumped all over. Chairs were turned on their sides, papers were everywhere. The floor was covered in white paper, Galleria brochures, and a million other office supplies. Someone broke in.

SCANDALOUS

Jack's gaze narrowed, surveying the damage before he said, "Stay here. " He took off into the back. I heard his footfalls disappear, leaving me in silence.

I flipped through the papers on the desk and the floor. They were random things to dump out, and when I pulled open the drawers, they weren't empty. When Jack came back he was fuming. He held the Tiffany's boxes in his hands and threw them on the desk. They landed with a thud.

"Stolen?" I asked. That jewelry was worth a small fortune. Anything from Tiffany's was.

He shook his head, "No. That's the problem. Something was taken, Abby, and they did this so I wouldn't be able to tell what it was." I looked around. The place was such a mess that it would take hours, possibly days, before it was all put back so we could tell what was gone.

"Call the cops, Jack. Tell them you have someone..."

His shoulders were tense. He snapped, dragging his hands through his hair as he looked around, "Tell them what? That one of my employees was messy? They didn't break in, Abby. They had a fucking key." Turning swiftly, he slammed his fist into the wall behind him. I winced. He looked over at me, "I wanted tonight to be perfect." He shook his head, "I'm sorry."

Walking to him, I stopped in front of him, and he wrapped his arms around me, "Tonight was perfect, Jack. It was completely perfect." He looked down at me, pressing a kiss to the top of my head. "Let's sift through this stuff and figure out what they took. And in the meantime, call the locksmith and change every lock on this building, change every code, every combination, until you figure out who's doing this to you."

———————

I called Kate and told her I was staying over. Her response was typical Kate, "If you sleep with him, you'll lose your job, Abby. Tell me that you guys are just playing house, and not fucking each other's brains out."

"Kate," I gasped, looking at the phone.

"Abby, tell me you didn't! I recognize that tone, young lady..."

I snorted into the phone, "Young lady? Are you insane? Fine. I'll tell you fast, but when Jack comes back I'm hanging up on you without another word.

Yes, I've been sleeping with him all week. No one else is here. He's having some business issues and we came home tonight after dinner and found out that someone broke in and stole something. We don't know what yet." Kate started to groan, obviously stuck on the first thing I said. I could hear Jack's footfalls getting closer, "And Kate... he proposed. I said yes. You are going to wear the most hideous bridesmaid's dress I can find. Not only will it have a big butt bow, but I'm going to make you wear a tiara on your head." I clicked END CALL and put the phone down right as Jack walked into the room. He noticed the huge smile on my face.

"What's my beautiful girl grinning about?" he asked. His arms were full of gear. He'd been sorting through boxes, trying to figure out what was missing. It was well past midnight and I was totally useless with this task. Only Jack would know what was missing.

Holding my arms behind my back, I grinned at him, "Oh, nothing. Just teasing Kate. She was being awful so I told her she was going to be the ugliest bridesmaid ever. Then I hung up on her."

Jack grinned as I giggled. He dropped his gear and walked back toward me, draping his hands around my waist, he pulled me close, "Abby, that was evil," he said totally deadpan, then added, "and hysterical. Kate's still crazy, right? She's still the anti-dress, I-hate-girlie-crap girl that she used to be, isn't she?"

I burst out laughing, nodding, "Yup!" My phone buzzed. Kate's number lit up the screen.

Watching me, he asked, "Are you going to answer that?"

I shook my head slowly, my fingers trailing along his collar, feeling the skin underneath. He blinked slowly, as if trying to focus, "Then let's do something else. I can find out what's missing in the morning." With that he swept his hand under me, and cradled me in his arms. I could feel every curve of his strong chest pressing against me. Jack moved out of the studio, through a door that connected to the outside. He held me, kissing me softly, as he rounded the studio to a small cottage—his home.

He fumbled with the knob, but got it open and carried me inside. "Stay with me tonight? No work, no studio. Just me and you, in my bed?" His voice was deep, his words traveling through me and making me feel weak.

I nodded. The cottage was like a studio apartment. It had a kitchenette and a big white bed. Everything was white. White on white on white. Jack lowered me onto the bed, kissed my head, and stood. Looking down at me, he pulled his shirt over his head, saying, "This was supposed to be the studio. I flipped things because I wanted the gallery and the studio together. It's kind of small for the two of us, but we can do anything you like to it. This is your home now, Abby. This is our bed. And you're going to be my wife." As he spoke, he removed his clothing all the while keeping his hot gaze on mine. When his eyes slide over my prone form, he smiled like he couldn't help it.

"It's perfect, Jack." And it was. The cottage felt like the perfect beach house. I loved that I could see the ocean and hear the waves. I loved the light linens and the softness of the room. As Jack undressed, I couldn't take my eyes off of him.

"There's one thing I'd like to add," he purred. My heart kicked up the pace, beating faster.

"What's that?" my voice hitched. Jack was completely naked and very turned on. I couldn't take my eyes off the hard temptation on his lower body. I sucked my lower lip without realizing it.

Jack leaned down, kissing me deeply before he pulled away and said, "There's a painting that I want to hang up in here. And maybe a few of those photographs of you, my goddess."

Glancing up at him, his words broke through my lusty haze. "The painting is done? The one of me from before…"

He nodded, "From before you tempted me and ensnared me in your wanton ways?" A sexy smile lined his full lips. "Yup, that one. The canvas is rolled up in a tube under the bed. It's yours, Abby. And it's stunning."

Smiling fully, I reached for him and embraced Jack, feeling every inch of his smooth skin against mine. The little dress I was wearing suddenly seemed very restricting. I moved to take it off, but Jack stopped me. "Let me be the one to do that," he leaned in close, kissing my neck, his hands pulling me tightly against him.

I groaned, feeling heat building inside of me, my knees growing weaker by the moment. "What do you like, Jack? Tell me…"

His lips pulled away from my neck. He took me by my hands, throwing a few pillows on the floor, and said, "Kneel." I did as he asked, my breathing growing more ragged by the moment. His smooth, firm length was in front of my mouth and I wanted it. I wanted to taste him and suck on him. My lips parted, my tongue licking my teeth as I openly stared. "Kiss me, Abby. Any way you want. Anything that feels good, do it." I glanced up at him, wide-eyed. He reached for my hair, stroking it gently as my face neared his most private parts.

Leaning my head against his stomach, I closed my eyes and breathed. The scent was divine. It filled my head, making me want him in my mouth even more. Brushing him over my lips, I kissed him gently. Holding onto his length, I rubbed him across my face, my eyes, my cheeks, before taking him in my mouth. Jack gasped as my lips closed around him. The heat that was building in my belly was so intense, so hot, that as I wrapped my tongue around Jack, I could feel the dampness between my legs. Jack's hands were in my hair, holding me, tugging gently as he moaned with each kiss. My lips slid over him, around him, up and down until Jack gasped, pushing me away, saying, "Oh God. Abby, I won't last long if you do that."

With his hands on my shoulders, I fixated on his beautiful erection before my eyes. "I want to taste, Jack." Leaning in, I pressed my lips to him again, then took him in my mouth. His fingers threaded through my hair as we fell into a rhythm, rocking and moaning. Every part of my body felt alive and hot. I wanted his hands on me, but I wanted to taste him more. Gently sucking and twisting my tongue around him, I moved my lips over him, loving him, tasting him. The grip on my hair tightened as Jack filled my mouth. The salty-sweet flavor slid over my tongue and down my throat. I devoured every last drop, licking my lips when there was no more.

Jack watched me, his dark eyes wide and sated until I licked my lips like I wanted more. With that, he bent down and lifted me, picking me up in his arms. "Abby, you have no idea what you're doing to me," he breathed heavily in my ear. His perfect body was pressed against me, but I wanted him closer.

"I want to feel you against me." His eyes met mine, shining like twin lakes. His fingers deftly unbuttoned and unzipped, as he pushed away fabric, revealing pale skin beneath. Every touch of his hands made me want more. I moaned, my head hanging back.

Jack lifted me onto the bed, "Tell me what you want, Abby." But I didn't know. I wanted everything, everywhere. I writhed as he watched me; his breath slipping over my hot bare skin. A single thought broke through the haze. More than anything, I wanted to feel him between my legs.

"Ride me, Jack. I want to feel you inside of me." Jack lowered his body next to mine on the bed, whispering in my ear, kissing my neck as his hand was splayed across my stomach, drifting slowly south.

"Anything you want," he breathed. His fingers lowered, touching between my legs, stroking me gently. My bottom rose off the bed, wanting to feel his touch as it disappeared, "You're so wet." His hand moved over me again, stroking, touching, pinching and rubbing. My head was spinning. Jack made me so lustful that I couldn't think.

Again his hands moved over me, in me, around me. I reeled, spreading my legs further, calling his name, "Jack." His fingers thrust inside me, pushing hard. Then he slid them up, touching my stomach, passing over my breasts, forming a line that went to my mouth. When he reached my lips, Jack ran his finger over my lips and then lowered his head, tasting me as he kissed me. His tongue swept over my lips, licking it all away. As I kissed him, I could taste it and something about him doing that made me hotter. My legs ached to hold him against me, but Jack moved slowly, teasing and tasting. His lips touched every inch of my body, lingering on my breasts, gently pinching my nipples, making me cry out. By the time he climbed on top of me, I wanted nothing but to feel him sliding into me, hard—over and over again.

When he said, "Be still, Abby. Let me feel you," I nearly died. Body rigid, I laid on the bed, fingers clawing the sheets, trying to control myself when I had no control left. Eyes shut tight, I felt Jack, hard and long, pushing into me. He'd do it slowly once, then withdraw and do it again. My chest thrust up toward him as I tried to remain still, aching, wanting to be touched. Jack's hands kneaded me gently, tugging my nipples when he pushed into me. His voice cut through the haze, "Look at me, Abby. I want to see your eyes."

Peeling my eyes open, I looked up at him. His hands were on my breasts, his hard body buried deep inside of me. I arched my back, trying not to move, watching him straddling me, looking down at me like I was everything he ever wanted. "I want you, Jack. Please, please..." I whispered, gazing into his eyes. The plea seemed to shatter him. My loving, teasing, Jack, suddenly withdrew and slammed into me hard. Gasping, I moaned, holding tight to his hips with my legs. He repeated the motion several times, each time faster and harder than the last. When he paused, I gasped, "More. Please, don't stop." Things blurred together, our intertwined bodies moving as one. Jack's glistening skin and dark eyes watched me. I could feel his gaze on my face as I cried out every time he pushed into me. Deeper and harder he pushed, taking me higher and higher.

"Come for me, Abby," Jack said, not stopping, thrusting into me hard and fast. His words, his voice, Tingling and wet, I could feel the gentle pulsating increase until I shattered into a million happy pieces. Jack felt it, moving harder, faster. He arched his back, pushing into me slowly, one last time, ready to pull out, but I asked him to stop.

Hands on the small of his back, I said, "Stay," and he did. Every small throb clung around his spent body, feeling him and making me happier and happier. Looking up at him, he watched me as the perfect pulses dulled.

Sliding next to me, he pulled my sweat soaked body on his chest, kissing my head. "I love you, Abby." And I fell asleep in perfect bliss.

CHAPTER TWENTY-NINE

The sun shone through the windows, waking me. Jack was awake, looking down at me, his hands playing with a stray curl. "Good morning, lover," he smiled. I smiled, snuggling closer to him when I heard something. Turning, I glanced at the door.

"Did you hear that?" I asked.

He nodded. "Yeah, I did." He slid out of bed, and pulled on his jeans. I watched the denim slide over his perfect ass, admiring the view as Jack walked to the window, peeking between the shutters. "Shit," he muttered, shaking his head. He looked back at me, worry in his eyes.

Sitting up, I clutched the sheet to my chest. "What is it?" My stomach sank, the afterglow from last night gone.

"Paparazzi and cop cars. Throw something on. The cops are headed to the door." Jumping out of bed, I scavenged the room for my panties and bra, putting them on fast. I'd only worn them for an hour or so, but I still wanted clean clothes. Clothes that I couldn't get to without going into the studio where my bag was. I donned the dress over my head and smoothed my hair just as the knocking came. Jack looked back at me and I nodded for him to open it.

Two officers and a guy in a suit pressed into the room, slamming the door shut. Jack reached for his shirt, and pulled it over his head as the police entered the tiny apartment. I leaned against the counter in the kitchenette, heart pounding. Something was wrong.

"Jack Gray, I'm afraid we aren't here with good news. If you'll finish getting dressed, I need you to come with us." The man in the dark suit spoke calmly, his eyes meeting Jack's. He was slightly leaner and taller than Jack, a blonde mustache clinging to his top lip.

"Nate," Jack replied, "What's this about? Why is the press camped on my front lawn?"

Nate ignored his question, nodding at me, "Abigail Tyndale?" I nodded. "You'll be coming with us also." One of the uniformed officers moved toward me, reaching around to remove the handcuffs from his belt.

Jack stepped between us, stopping the man, "What the fuck is going on? Nate?" he looked at the guy in the suit, fury glowing in his eyes. "Are we under arrest?"

Nate nodded. There was sympathy in his voice, "Listen, Jack. Someone steam-plowed you. Evidence came in last night that your studio isn't what we thought."

"What the hell do you think it is?" Tension lined Jack's body.

"I can't talk to you, Jack. I would have come without the press, but someone tipped them off. You've been accused of running a prostitution ring, and Miss Tyndale is your newest girl."

My jaw fell open. For the first time, I talked, "What?" My voice came out in a rush, more forceful than I'd intended. "You think I'm a hooker?"

"The charge is trading sexual favors for money. I have to remove you both from the premises in handcuffs. I'm sorry, Jack." The man in the suit waved to the officers to cuff us.

Jack's eyes were wide. He didn't move away from me, "Nate, this is Belinda's shit. You can't possibly believe her? She's been trying to screw me for years!"

Nate turned to Jack, shaking his head, "Last night other girls gave testimonies about their association with you and your company, Jack. It's not Belinda. A judge already signed the arrest warrants. You think we'd come in here empty handed and risk you suing our asses off?" He shook his head. "Jack, this looks bad. Your accounts have been frozen, your studio and all its contents are being confiscated. Someone has you by the balls. You're fucked, my friend. Call your lawyer, but I can't do more than that. My hands are tied and people are watching. I can't make exceptions for you or I'll catch hell for it."

Every muscle in Jack's body was corded tight, like he was going to explode. Fear was choking me into silence. I watched the silver cuffs in the cop's hand as Jack called his lawyer. The last thing he said was, "Get Abby's name out of this and make it so it never happened." He looked up at me, after hanging up. "I'm sorry, Abby. We have to go."

I shook my head, not wanting to make things harder than they already were. I held out my wrists. The cold metal bit into my skin. The officer started to lead me to the door, but Jack spoke, "Take her out the back. Nate, please. This has nothing to do with her. Even if I clear my name, you know what happens to women accused of this shit. It sticks. Don't feed her to the press. Nate." Jack spoke to him like they were friends, like they knew each other.

Nate turned his brown eyes to me, then back to Jack, "Someone's got to go out the front, Jack."

Jack held his wrists up, "Done. Take me out the front. Now." The cop put his hand on my back, leading me to the back door. There were still people there, but everyone would be watching the front door when Jack stepped out. "I'll fix this, Abby. I promise." The suit and the cop pushed Jack through the front door. Camera flashes and people yelling, asking questions, wafted through the empty room. The cop waited half a beat and then ushered me through the backdoor. I held my head low, hands cuffed in front, as he opened the squad car and helped me inside. The cop didn't speak. Just as he closed the door, I heard it. The press turned and saw me leaving in another car. Questions were hurling at us, but the cop started the car and drove away.

Everything after that was a blur. Tears stung my eyes, making it impossible to see. Someone read me my rights, I was fingerprinted, photographed, and read my charges. Prostitution. My stomach sank. A female officer repeated herself, "Do you know what's happening to you? Do you know where you are? Do you understand what you're being charged with?" I shook my head slowly, afraid to look at her. The holding cells around me were filled with men, all of who looked depraved and murderous. I could feel their eyes on my body, watching me. The cop that brought me in escorted me out of that area and into the back. He unlocked a cell door and I stepped inside. My heart sank as I heard it clunk shut behind me. It was everything I could manage to not cry. This place terrified me.

Before I turned around, a familiar voice rang in my ears, "So you weren't the mole after all."

CHAPTER THIRTY

I turned around and saw Linda sitting on a bench. She was the only person in the cell. Relief flooded through me. "Linda, what are you doing here?"

Dark bags clung under her eyes, "I'm an accomplice in Long Island's elite prostitution ring, or so I've been told." Her arms were folded over her chest, her head tilted back against the wall. "And what's your crime? Actually hooking? Or something else?"

I sat down hard next to her, "Hooker." Staring at the floor, I felt the rage I'd been repressing bubble up inside of me. "Who did this to him, Linda?"

"Don't know, hun." She crossed her ankles, her slacks completely wrinkled. "For a while, I thought it was you. When you came back is when all this crap came to the surface." She shook her head, "Obviously I've changed my theory since you're sitting next to me. But whoever it was, they planned everything perfectly. This will damn him, ruin his career and he'll lose everything—every penny. The government will seize it as ill-gotten gains."

My mouth hung open. I stared at her, "I don't understand how someone could do this. How could they toss away three lives like this? My reputation is gone, so is yours. And Jack, oh my God... " I shook my head, lowering it into my hands.

"None of us saw it coming. And whoever did it somehow sweet-talked a judge into signing arrest warrants without physical proof."

My stomach sank, "He said they have proof."

Linda closed her eyes and let out a rush of air. She leaned forward and put her face in her hands.

"Shit. We're fucked, Abby. All of us." She sat back, looking at me, "What proof? Paper? Testimony?"

"It sounded like both. Linda, think—who would do this to him? Who hates him that much?"

The older woman shook her head, her eyes glassy. "I don't know, hun. I just don't know."

The jailer called my name, "Abigail Tyndale, you made bail. Please step over to the bars." I looked back at Linda. "How long have you been here?"

"About 14 hours, now," she replied, leaning back against the wall, kicking her feet out. Thinly contained rage played out on her face.

"Jack doesn't know you're here. I'll make sure they get you out fast." The woman didn't answer. She stared straight ahead, nodded once, and continued to gaze at the cinderblock wall like she was willing it to explode.

I walked out of the cell and through the back of the jail to a car waiting out back. It was a sleek black Beamer. The jailer opened the door and I was pushed inside. Jack wasn't there. The door slammed shut. Instead, there was a handsome man with mocha skin and a slick suit sitting next to me. A phone was pressed to his ear and he was saying, "His assets are frozen and he's not a flight risk, Kenny. What the fuck are they doing?" He uh-huhed a few times and snapped his phone shut. The car lurched forward.

"Miss Tyndale, I wish we could have met under better circumstances." He held out his hand and I took it. Shaking it, he said, "Phil Green, Mr. Gray's lawyer." I wanted to ask him what happened, where Jack was. As if he could read my face, he said, "I'll fill you in on the way. Jack's fine, but he's still in holding. His assets were frozen and his bail amount supersedes his liquid assets. I have to move a few things, and he should be out in a few hours." It felt like I was kicked in the stomach. Jack in jail with those people for hours? "You were easier to extract, lower bail."

"Linda is in there too." I added. "I'm sure Jack doesn't know. Can we get her out too?"

Phil nodded, writing something on a tablet. "See anyone else in there? Gus, maybe?"

I shook my head. "So Gus did this?"

The lawyer shrugged, "Since he's the only one not in jail, it stands to reason."

I sat back as we drove to Kate's apartment. I groaned when I saw the press camped out in front of the building. Phil said, "I'll get you inside. Try to wait it out and they'll go away. The first three days will suck, but if you don't give them anything, they leave.

If you give them more stuff to feed off of, they'll never leave. Understand?" He spoke to me directly, like I was traumatized. I nodded, hating every moment of this. "Your roommate is already aware of this and will open the door for you. Go straight inside. Jack will be in touch."

"Is there anything I can do?" I asked. This felt so hopeless.

Phil shook his head, "I'm afraid not. Jack's fucked every way 'til Tuesday. They have models saying he slept with them—they signed affidavits. Combine that with the surveillance on you two for the past few days, and..."

I blanched, "What? They were watching us?"

Phil shook his head, "It's damning, Abby. Jack's not going to recover from this."

"Then why are you helping him?" I asked point blank.

"I owe him a favor, one huge-ass favor. He called it in." Phil slid designer sunglasses on his nose and pushed open his door. He stood and buttoned his coat like he was posing for GQ. Cameras swarmed the car, but he held up his hand pushing them back. He quickly opened my door, pushing me through the crowd to the door. Someone yelled slut. Kate threw the door open and pulled me inside.

Tears welled up in my eyes, and huge sobs came out of my mouth. I couldn't stop them. Things were beyond repair.

CHAPTER THIRTY-ONE

Kate was doting. She helped me calm down before showing me the papers. Jack was on every cover with words like corrupt, prostitution ring, and scandalous. I didn't want to read them, but someone tipped off the press. "These were run before the arrest this morning?" I asked Kate.

She nodded, "Yeah, probably late last night. See there's no mention of the arrest in the printed copies.

The online papers added it to the stories when it happened." After a moment, she asked, "Abby, is there any way it's true?" I glared at her like she was the stupidest person alive. "They're saying he paid you for sex. That he's done it before."

Staring at the papers, I answered, "He proposed, Kate."

"He's been doing scandalous things with you for the past week, Abby. Is there any chance that you misunderstood..."

I cut her off, "No! There's no way I missed the nonverbal hooker cue, Kate! I'm not that stupid and he's not like that!" Why did people keep underestimating me? It was like they saw a dumb hick, and not the highly educated New Yorker.

Without looking at me, she asked, "Where's the ring? He proposed, so where is it?"

My stomach twisted as I stroked my ring finger, "We were going to go and pick one out today."

"That story, what he said, Abby," she shoved a newspaper in front of me, "it lines up with the testimony of another employee. She said she was his sex toy, that he promised to marry her, and then fired her. She admits to trading sexual favors for money. She said her official job description was Jonathan Gray's assistant."

All the blood drained from my face. I picked up the paper and looked at it, trying to find the name of the assistant. "Kate, who said this? Why didn't they name the source?"

"Abby, stop. Accept this for what it was," her hand clasped mine. Her eyes were wide, concerned. "He used you. He got busted. Don't make it worse than it already is by holding him up on a pedestal and denying the obvious."

Tears were streaming down my cheeks. I shook my head, "It's not true, Kate. He loves me." But the papers surrounding me all told the same story; wealthy Jonathan Gray made his fortune by having sex with his models, capturing them in the throes of ecstasy, and photographing their illicit acts. He later painted the images of the women, claiming to have been inspired. More models were coming forward, telling the same story—they traded sex for a referral, for money, for fame--with Jonathan Gray.

CHAPTER THIRTY-TWO

Kate unplugged the phone to end the ceaseless barrage of reporters. She gazed out the window, long hair down her back. "There seems to be less of them today." I nodded, staring vacantly. She turned to me. "This'll pass, Abby."

I looked up at her from my spot on the couch, legs tucked under me. I didn't know what to believe about Jack. It was easy to say one person was lying— that one person would perjure herself—but five models came forward in the past twenty-four hours, all saying the same story. It made me sick. I sat in the living room all night, unable to sleep. The TV glowed in front of me, but I couldn't watch. Everything was about me.

The news person was saying, "More pictures of Miss Tyndale have been leaked showcasing the perversion of this once elite studio." They posted a picture of me from the photo shoot, blurring certain parts to make it acceptable for TV. I felt like I was going to puke. Kate grabbed the remote and turned it off.

"You don't need to hear that," she sat down in her chair. I didn't move, didn't blink. "Abby, Phil's been trying to get hold of you. He said he was coming later, bringing Jack with him." I glanced at her. "I told him I didn't want that son-of-a-bitch here, but it has something to do with clearing your name. So I said he could come. Do you want me to stay?" She was hesitant, like she suspected there was lava boiling beneath my calm facade, ready to explode.

I nodded once, not looking at her. Jack. I couldn't believe that he used me. I couldn't believe that I fell for his lies. I'd known him for so long, at least I thought I did. It was clear that this wasn't the work of Belinda. It looked like Jack was just a pervert who got caught with his hand in the cookie jar—and I was the cookie jar.

"What do I say to him, Kate?" It was the first thing I'd said since our conversation yesterday. "I feel so completely used," tears streamed down my face. "He knew what he was doing, what would happen to me when he was done, and he did it anyway. The papers said he was doing the same thing to me that he did to the others." I shook my head slowly. Life had taken on a surreal feeling and I'd gone numb trying to cope.

"Don't think about that right now, Abby. Just save yourself, and we'll pick up the pieces." I didn't look at her. Kate moved in front of me, took my hands in hers and said, "You'll get through this." But I didn't believe her. It felt like I was dead on the inside, a walking corpse.

The knock on the door startled me. I couldn't stand the thought of facing Jack. "Sit. I'll get it." Kate opened the door quickly. Jack and Phil walked in. Kate moved next to me protectively. "Say what you want and get out." She was forceful, like a mama protecting her young.

I could sense Jack looking at me, watching my face. Tears continued to stream from my eyes. I was unable to stop them. "Abby?" he said, not coming closer because of Kate. "I have something that will clear your name."

Slowly, I turned my face up to see him. He looked like hell, dark circles under his eyes like he hadn't slept since it happened. The last time he rested must have been when I was in his arms. My stomach churned like I had eaten glass. Swallowing hard, I asked, "Is it true? Just tell me, Jack. Was I so naïve that I couldn't see what you were doing?"

He looked away, arms folding over his chest. He nodded once. Kate's fist curled like she would hit him, but Phil spoke, breaking the nasty glare that Jack was getting. "Miss Tyndale, if you sign this paper, you walk away from this whole thing with no record. We've spoken with the state, and based on your previous experience with things like this, they'll strike everything and let you walk."

I eyed him suspiciously, "Why would they do that?"

"Because you would be the final nail in the coffin," he sighed, rubbing his head like he didn't want to say it, "of Jonathan Gray. If you attest to your acts as being of mutual consent and being too inexperienced to realize what Jack had offered you, they'll clear your name."

I glanced at Jack. Something didn't sound right. "Jack didn't offer me anything like that." Jack's blue eyes lifted, meeting mine. "What are you doing? You lied to me once, don't do it again."

Jack's arms were folded tightly across his chest, "Sign it, Abby. You didn't understand what I offered. The others did." He looked me in the eye when he said it, but something was wrong. I could feel it. He was tense, mad, but not at me. Desperation oozed from him, thick, choking him.

I stood and walked over to him, looking into his eyes, "Tell me that you lied. Tell me that you don't love me, and I'll sign it."

Jack's lips formed a thin pink line, his shoulders practically shaking. "I don't love you. I said those things to get you to do what I wanted, what I needed for my work." His voice was cold, each word dripping with disdain.

Kate's hand was on my shoulder, pulling me toward the counter, "Sign it, Abby." She shoved a pen into my hand.

I looked at Phil, "What happens if I don't sign? What will they do with me?"

He glanced at Jack, as if asking permission before saying, "Then you'll be the only model who didn't bargain out, and the last one standing takes the fall. There will be jail time, Miss Tyndale. There has to be a public fall of those accused. The scandal is too large for this to go away quietly. It's in your best interest to sign the paper."

I glanced at it, feeling the plastic pen in my hand. I flicked the pen on the counter, and said, "No. I'm not signing. I'm not that stupid, and if I was, I deserve what I get." I glared at Jack. His arms loosened, like he was melting as I shoved past him, walking down the hallway and slamming the door to my room.

CHAPTER THIRTY-THREE

When I came out later, they were gone, but the papers were still there. The pen was still sitting there, ready to be used. Kate was making dinner, soup from the looks of it. It smelled wonderful, but I didn't feel like eating. I sat on a chair, looking at her. "Would you have signed it?"

She turned around, a boiling pot in front of her. "I honestly don't know. I'd want to do what was right, but I'd want to save my ass more." I nodded, shoulders slumped, sitting on a stool. Kate said, "You have a way of doing what's right, even if it kills you. Why'd you say no?"

I shrugged, "It felt wrong. Something's wrong with the whole thing. I just don't know what. It's possible that it's me, that I'm a moron. Jack pretty much told me so, but I can't sign that."

Kate smiled sadly, "I wish you would, but I'm also glad you didn't."

I nodded. Kate turned back to the pot. "Did he say anything else, before he left?"

She dipped a spoon into the boiling broth, raising it to her lips. She blew on it gently before sipping it. Nodding, she banged a spoon on the side of the pot and said, "As a matter of fact, he did. He said, "make sure she signs this." Not the kind of thing a jackass would say. If you sign that paper, his case is screwed. Did you read it?" I shook my head, glancing at the pages. "The other evidence is only testimony. Your case is the only one that holds tangible proof to the accusations. If you sign that, Jack loses everything and goes to jail for a very long time."

My stomach twisted as I picked up the papers, staring at them. I wouldn't survive in jail. I knew that without a doubt. I was too soft, too sensitive. It made me a target, but it also made me see things others missed. And this, I could feel it—Jack was lying—it just wasn't the lie I thought.

———————

I parked Kate's car at the Econolodge. Rain was pouring from the sky like someone left a hose on. I stepped from the dry interior and was instantly soaked. The dark parking lot made me nervous, but I crossed to the door with the golden number 34. I banged on it twice. Loudly.

Jack pulled the door open, his jaw dropping to his chest, surprised to see me. "Abby, what are you...?"

But I didn't give him a chance to answer, "How could you look me in the eye and lie to my face?" Taking my soaking wet hands, I shoved his chest. "Answer me! Don't I deserve as much?" Rain pelted me, soaking me through and through. Water dripped down my face, but Jack didn't touch me.

"You deserve more than I can give. Go home, Abby. Sign the paper," his voice was cold. Moving back, Jack started to close the door. Kicking my foot out, I stuck it in the jam before the door shut.

"I'm already a martyr, Jack. Your compassion is wasted on me. I've been fired from my church, they were all too happy to do it. There's nothing left for me. I might as well throw myself off a bridge or go rot in jail. It makes no difference at this point. What I want to know is how you can stand there and lie to me? Answer me Jack, or so help me, I'll..."

Jack yelled back, the sound of the rain filling the air, "Or you'll what, Abby? I tried to save you. I can't do a damn thing to help me, but I can clear your name. I can remove it from your record and give you another chance." He stepped closer to me, rain pouring down his neck, soaking his shirt. "Sign the fucking papers."

As he was yelling at me, something snapped. I couldn't stand it anymore, "You can't save me, Jack! You can't save someone who doesn't want to be saved! And I don't want it. I'll do what I have to, even if it kills me. I am not signing that fucking paper. I am not accusing you of something you didn't do, but for the life of me, I can't understand why you won't admit it!" I pulled the papers out of my jacket, and ripped it in half, shredding it. Every ounce of anger that flowed through me was put into that action. The silent volcano within me exploded. I was screaming at Jack, and when he reached for the paper, trying to stop me, I threw it at him. The only thing keeping me from a jail cell was ripped to shreds, sticking to the parking lot like wet confetti.

Jack was shocked, watching me rant like a lunatic, shredding my freedom and tossing it in the air like it didn't matter. "Words won't save me. What I say makes no difference. Someone did this to me, and there's no going back. Even if Phil clears my name and I avoid jail, I'm ruined." He pushed his sopping wet hair out of his eyes. "There's nothing left here for you, Abby. I'm screwed no matter what I do. I just hoped that I could make things better for you."

My chest was heaving, huge tears of rage dripping down my face, making a hot trail. "What's mine is yours, Jack. The good, the bad, and the ugly. All of it. I said yes when you asked me to marry you. I knew what that meant. I'm not here for your money. I don't care about your studio. I'm here for you. I was here when things were good, and I'm here when they've gone to hell."

His eyes were glassy, but he didn't step out closer. A sad smile snaked across his lips, "This is one time that I wish to God you'd listen to me. Go home, Abby. Wash your hands of me."

The door closed in my face. Jack vanished on the other side, leaving me standing alone in the rain. It felt like my heart died in my chest. I couldn't breathe. I didn't know what to do, so I stood there, rain pelting me, soaking me to the bone. Minutes passed. Dread pooled in my stomach, sickeningly quick. It felt like the cold night would swallow me whole and I wished it would. It would be easier than this—easier than leaving him behind. That's when I realized that I couldn't do it. Jack was trying to save me, and I was trying to save him.

Determination sprang up my spine. I moved closer to his door, trying to get out of the rain, and sat down. About an hour passed. The eaves weren't wide enough to keep me dry. My numb eyes stared at the rain, falling from heaven, washing away everything that hurt me. Thoughts drifted into my mind, and I wondered what I'd do if Jack opened the door and turned me away. Refusing to sign those papers was suicide, but it felt like I was already dead. The wind blew, pelting the cold water into my face. My head was against the jam, coat pulled up around my neck, pressing my face away from the wind, toward the door when the knob turned. Jack pulled the door open and I fell backward into the room, soaking wet.

For a moment, I lay on my back, stunned, looking up into his sad eyes. "Abby," was all he said as he stepped over me.

There was a moment after I stood up when I just stared at him before I found my voice. I found a part of me that I didn't know I had. It was ferocious and scared the hell out of me. Maybe it was my fight or flight instinct kicking in. I don't know, but what I did know was that I wasn't giving Jack up without a fight.

Folding my arms across my chest, I repressed a shiver, saying, "Send me away, Jack. Lie to my face. Tell me that you did horrible things when I know you didn't. I'll just come back..." my teeth were chattering. The muscle in my jaw tensed trying to control it. "I promised I wouldn't leave you. I'm not breaking my promise to save my own ass."

Jack's lips parted like he was going to say something, but Phil's black car zoomed into the parking lot and stopped in front of us. Jack glanced at me one last time before he pulled the motel door shut. Brushing past me, heading directly for the car door Phil kicked open from inside. Jack leaned into the car and emerged with a manila envelope. Without a word, he tossed it to me. Stunned at his cold behavior, I fumbled it and nearly dropped the thing on the wet ground. Clutching it, I looked down at the package. It was getting soaked.

Jack glared at me, his eyes filled with loathing, "Sign it. Get this back to Phil by tonight. There's no silver lining. There's no other way out. We're through, Abby." There was no bite in his voice. It almost sounded like an apology. His eyes locked with mine, staring vacantly, "I used you. Get over it." He turned his back to me and slid into Phil's car. The door slammed and they drove away, leaving me sopping wet, standing in the parking lot of the Econolodge with a yellow envelope as my only salvation.

CHAPTER THIRTY-FOUR

Kate used vacation days to stay with me. Or maybe she didn't want to shove her way through the paparazzi. Anyway, she was home and awake when I trudged in soaked to the bone.

Her dark hair was tied in a knot, forming a make-shift ponytail of sorts. She wore gray sweats and fuzzy socks, opposed to her normally perfectly pressed work attire. She was munching on a bowl of Cheerios. "Tell me you didn't." Her spoon stopped half way to her mouth as she stared, slack jawed at my drowned rat look. Hastily, she put her bowl down and ran over to me, "Abby, that ass doesn't deserve this kind of loyalty from you." She took my hand, and started peeling me out of my soaked jacket, "You're frozen!" Her hands grabbed my wrist, feeling how cold my skin was. "Shit, Abby. You'll catch your death!"

While she scolded me for being so stupid, I stared blankly. My mind was reeling, working double time. I felt like I was missing something. Before I knew what was happening, Kate was snapping her fingers under my nose, trying to get my attention. "What?" I asked like she hadn't said a word.

She cocked her head at me, concern on her face, "When are you going to see the way the world works? Your entire life has been like this—one train wreck after another. You can't walk around trying to save everyone. It only ensures a short and painful life for you." She threw a blanket over my shoulders. Nodding her head, she indicated that I should follow her down the hall. Kate pushed open the bathroom door and turned on the shower. Within seconds steam filled the air and my shivering lessened.

I rolled my eyes, "You sound like my mother."

"Good!" she huffed, hands on her hips. "Then maybe I'll get through to you!"

Kate meant well, but she didn't know. My family looked picture perfect on the outside, but on the inside it was an all-American mess. "That wasn't a compliment. My mother was faithfully silent, moving through life trying to make the least amount of waves possible. Someone wronged her, she looked the other way. Someone hurt me, she didn't make a sound. Nothing, Kate. She didn't lift a finger when my Dad was drunk out of his mind, his hand smashing into my face. Why do you think I was allowed to stay at your house so much? It was the road of least conflict for her. She was a coward, Kate. That's why she's dead. That's why I don't have her anymore. It wasn't a fluke that my Dad was drunk when their car crashed. I'm just glad they didn't kill anyone else." My words were cold, and bitter. Kate's eyes widened as I spoke. She had no idea, and I'd never told her.

"I'm sorry, Abby. I just want to help. I don't want to see you hurt even more." She sighed, pushing her frizzing hair out of her face. The room was very warm now, sticky with steam. "The press caught your altercation with him. It's on the news. They're making fun of you, saying that the poor little preacher girl doesn't understand that the big bad city boy played her. Abby, you're making this worse by going to him. You have to stay away or this will never end. The paparazzi are like a flock of rabid pigeons and you're feeding them." Her tone had changed from chastising to pleading.

I nodded, "You're right about that. I won't do it again, but I can't sign the papers either."

"Take a shower Abby. Get warm, and hope to God that you didn't catch pneumonia. I'll heat up some soup for you." She turned and left.

Wiping the steam from the mirror, I looked at my face in the glass. My auburn hair was plastered to my head. Thick black lines smudged under my eyes and my skin had developed a corpse-like pallor. I watched my face as the steam turned the mirror white once again. Resolve building in my sleep-deprived mind, I stood in the shower wondering who hated Jack with such venom.

———————

After a hellish night of no sleep, I pulled on my own sweats. I sat at the counter with Kate sipping soup. The rain continued to beat against the glass outside. The only perk was that there were fewer cameras today. "While I was sitting outside, I was thinking about something." She glanced at me, and I continued after sipping the scalding liquid. "Everyone was implicated—Gus, too."

Kate nodded, reaching for a paper, flipping through it. Her finger trailed down a list of names implicated in the scandal. Finally she said, "Yeah, Gus Peck was implicated, too. It doesn't mention if he was arrested or not. It looks like he pled out also, which damns Jack even more."

Looking at the soup, I stirred it with my spoon. It felt like a thought was there, something major, and just out of reach. My waterlogged brain skirted the idea last night—it's something about the arrests— something that's off. Or missing. I wondered, thinking out loud, hoping it would make sense at some point, "And everyone thought it was me, because all this crap started when I arrived."

Kate nodded, "Yeah, but Abby, they know you didn't do it. If Jack's innocent,"

I cut her off, stating it as a fact, "He is innocent."

"Fine. He is innocent. If that's the case, then someone played you guys. They watched you, and made sure they had everything they needed to string both of you up." She sipped from her coffee cup, "And you have no idea who it is?"

Shaking my head, I replied, "Belinda is the only person that seemed to have enough venom for Jack, but she didn't have a key. And unless she was working with someone, I don't see how this happened." Staring, swirling my spoon in my soup I muttered, "Time. The time is important." I was lost in thought, talking out loud. Kate leaned on the counter, looking at me. "Me, Belinda, the interviews, the sales girl, the assistant." When I said it, the thought sparked into a flame. "The assistant. Kate, was Emily arrested?"

Kate reached for the paper again, her finger running down the list of names. Shaking her head, she said, "No. There's no one on this list with that name." Lowering the paper she asked, "Maybe she pled out?"

I shook my head, "No, the cop in the suit—the police chief—said that they would make examples of anyone who didn't cooperate. He said they couldn't sweep this under the rug and deal with it quietly because the press already latched on. That's why Jack and I, and everyone else, were all arrested publically. He made a big deal about the public part. If Emily was implicated, her name would be on that list."

Kate dropped the paper, turning toward me on her seat, "So what are you thinking?"

"I'm thinking that everyone has been keeping an eye on the wrong girl."

CHAPTER THIRTY-FIVE

After some research a la Google, I found that Emily was still on Long Island. She didn't have a husband, well, not one that was living, and she didn't move.

"Well, strike one against Emily," Kate said, reading the screen over my shoulder. "Her husband died a while ago too. Even if she deluded herself, twenty years is a long time to keep the facade up." She glanced down at me, "So what are you thinking?"

Staring at the screen, I shrugged, "I have no idea. She seemed nice." I turned to Kate, draping my arm over the back of the chair, "She was there the first day I assisted Jack. Thinking about it, she seemed protective of him. She told me how important it was to keep an eye on Jack. That one word could bring his career crashing down."

"So? That doesn't mean she's the evil bitch that orchestrated this whole thing. What she said was true. Everyone in the art world knows Jonathan Gray and his erotic paintings. The thing that made them worth millions was his reputation. He was abstinent for so long that people thought he was gay."

"What?" my eyes flew open. It felt like my eyeballs were going to roll out of my head. Kate didn't seem to realize what she said.

Shrugging, she answered, "Everybody knows that, Abby. Jack didn't date anyone, which is why people were suspicious of him. He had very few relationships over the years. We were chomping at the bit, waiting for him to get caught with his pants down. No one is that good."

I stared blankly ahead. As she spoke, Jack's paintings appeared in my mind, one by one. The longing, the loneliness, the haunted sensation of being lost. I rubbed my hands over my eyes, "Kate.

His paintings... it's all in his paintings. He's really been alone all this time? He said he had a relationship with Belinda, though."

Kate shrugged, "It wasn't long enough for the press to pick up on it. Abby, we're getting off track. I realize this probably looks very romantic to you, but it's a feeding frenzy for the press. That's why they sunk their teeth into him—he's different, damaged, and the perfect way to boost ratings. They'll run with this till Doomsday if he goes to trial. If you sign those papers, Phil can plead him out."

"Where'd you hear that?" I asked. Phil didn't say that while he was here.

"The TV. Abby, the longer you hold out, the worse this gets. He told you to sign. Are you seriously going to keep this going?"

I shook my head. "No. I'm not." Turning back to the computer, I hit print. Emily's address and phone number were on a sheet of paper within seconds. "I'm going to check this out. Call Phil for me? Tell him I'll drop the papers by later tonight."

CHAPTER THIRTY-SIX

Kate thought I was insane, and told me so, but I had a feeling about this. Emily wasn't just an old lady. She lied like a sociopath. There wasn't a trace of remorse or an indication of anything when she spoke to me. She felt like the awesome aunt I never had. I looked at the address and then up at Emily's front door. She lived in a little cape, cute as a button, on a street in Cutchogue. Stepping out of the car, I grabbed my purse and slid my iPhone into the plastic holder on my jeans. It was bulky and messed with the outfit, but I didn't want the phone in my purse.

Before I knocked on the door, it swung open, "Abby, honey!" She smiled widely, gesturing me inside. "Come on in. It's so nice to see you."

"It's nice to see you too, Emily." Her house looked picture perfect. It was classic old lady, doilies and all. "I thought you were moving? I was so glad when I realized that you were still here." I tried to sound sweet, and wasn't sure how I was doing. I was a horrible liar.

She nodded, and I followed her into the living room. "Well, you know men. They say one thing, then do another." She turned suddenly, her fingers on her lips like she said something she shouldn't have. "I'm sorry, dear. That was thoughtless of me."

I shrugged it off, although the comment instantly made me think I was on the right trail since she was referring to husband again like he was alive and currently making decisions. A cold chill ran through me. I really hoped she wasn't the Norman Bates type of crazy. "It's all right. There isn't much you can say that would upset me these days. The press has been horrible." We sat at her oak table. She handed me a doily placemat.

"How about some tea, dear?"

I nodded, "Thank you very much."

As she started the kettle and grabbed two ancient tea cups, she asked, "So, what brings you up here?"

Distracted, I noticed a painting on the wall. It was small, but it was clearly one of Jack's. "I was hoping to speak to you about Jack, but Emily," she turned hearing the question in my voice, following my finger pointing at the painting, "is that one of Jack's?"

She laughed, nodding like a crazy old coot. "Yes, an early finger painting. Nothing more. Not worth anything. It's just a memento he gave me before I left." The painting was in a gold gilded frame. I wasn't an art connoisseur, but I knew better than to think it was worthless, even now. She added, "Nothing like the painting he made of you, or so I hear." She placed a tea cup in front of me. I picked up the bag and dipped it into the cup, watching the tea snake through the steaming water.

I blushed slightly, "Oh, that. It's nothing. He's made so many paintings. I don't see how that one would matter." I glanced at her out of the corner of my eye. Did she suspect me? Or did she think I was the innocent idiot the news made me out to be?

"Oh, honey!" she laughed, touching my hand. "Jack's paintings are all monochromatic, didn't you notice?" I shook my head like a moron. Duh, Abby no notice nothing. Wide-eyed, I looked at her over the top of my cup as I took a sip. I briefly wondered if she was crazy enough to poison me, but since she was drinking it too, I thought the tea was okay. "Well, that one is different. It's the last in his collection, the only one in color, and the only one that feels— hopeful. One day that'll fetch a pretty penny."

"Really?" I asked, shocked that she seemed to know anything. She rambled on like Kate, and the only reason Kate knew stuff was because of her connection to MOMA. "But the scandal. You really think it's still worth something?"

She shook her head. "Just between us girls, not in this lifetime. Even if Jack clears his name, which would be a miracle, his reputation will remain damaged. People don't forget things like this."

"No, they don't." Sipping my tea, I thought fast, or I tried to think fast. My brain felt like it was submerged in cement that was rapidly drying. Something was wrong here. Doilies, crazy old bat, Jack's painting, knowledge of art... I couldn't put my finger on it.

"I'm so sorry that this affected you too. Jack can be quite the charmer. I had no idea he was capable of something like this." Her shrewd eyes were on me. This was a test. I could feel it.

I played the too-innocent-to-be-alive card, "Neither did I. That's why I came out here. I wanted to ask you what I should do. They told me I can sign something that will damn Jack, but it'll get me off. I don't really have anyone to talk about this with." Emily watched me carefully. I threw in, "I really need someone to bounce things off of—someone who'd understand—someone who knows Jack." I put my cup down and buried my face in my hands. I was so going to Hell. Real tears streamed down my face. When Emily patted my shoulder, I glanced at her. She seemed to make up her mind.

"Oh, you are the most foolish girl I've ever met. No wonder your mother's dead. She probably wanted to get away from you." Her sweet old lady façade splintered as she spoke, more venom spewing from between the cracks as she talked.

My jaw dropped as more tears lined my face, "How can you say that?" My voice became thin and shrill.

Emily stood, and ripped my cup out of my hands. "If you have half a brain, do as I tell you. I know you're screwed and I feel kind of guilty for taking down a minister. I thought you'd fold first, not be the last moron standing." She yanked my chair out from under me, shoving me toward the door while she spoke. "Settle. Sign the damn papers. Then when Jack's things are put up for auction, go get one. This is my good deed for the day." She stopped me in front of the screen door, talking to me like I'd taken too many shots to the head. Hands on my shoulders she said, "Get yourself a few hundred dollars and buy a painting. That's all they'll be worth at the auction. Then hold onto it. People have short memories, and Jack's work defines a new movement in art. His pieces were the first in the post-modern Evokism Movement."

"What?" I gasped, jaw open. I wasn't playing dumb, anymore. I had no idea what she was talking about.

She shook me once, hard. "If you're too stupid to follow my directions, you deserve what you get. It's called Darwinism, Abby—or did they fail to teach you that concept at seminary. Now pay attention. Jack's name is mud, but in a few years it won't be, and his paintings will be in limited supply and high demand. Sell it then. Pay off your loans and go find some happy farmer to marry you." She tried to push me through the screen door, but I dug my heels in.

"Why did you do this to him? He trusted you. He thought of you like his mother! And you used everything you saw against him. How could you?"

A wicked smile spread across her lips, "Because I could. Jack didn't watch his back. It was his own damn fault. All those models were all too happy to comply after their arrests. Jack's auction will look like a group of misfits bidding on his crap so they can destroy it. And I hope to God that they do. That will make the paintings I have worth more. And we all know, money talks, darling. So do yourself a favor, and remember what I told you." She shoved me through the screen door.

Tripping over the threshold, I yelled, "I'll tell the cops what you did! That you set Jack up." I was seething. I spit the words between my teeth at her, my hands balled into fists at my sides. She destroyed Jack. She nearly destroyed me.

She laughed, "Hollow threats from a hooker. No one will believe you, girl. It'll just keep Jack's name in the paper longer, and make it that much harder for him. If you want to know the truth, this was fun. Much better than I thought it'd be," she laughed clasping her hands together. "For years I looked for dirt on Jack, but there was nothing. I couldn't get a thing on him. That bitch Belinda was the skeleton in his closet and I kept dragging her out, hoping he'd do something. But then you came along and I didn't have to. You're charming naivety worked perfectly. All those things Jack vowed to never do, he did with you. It was easy to tip off the press, report a prostitution ring to the cops after that."

"There is no prostitution ring!" I yelled stamping my foot like a child on her front lawn. It was undignified, but I didn't care at this point. Spill your guts Emily! My stompy feet only made her laugh harder.

"Of course not! There never was a prostitute at Jack's studio. The best lies are laced with truth my dear, saying the things that people want to hear. Thank you for your assistance. Now, get off of my lawn before I shoot you." She slammed the door with a loud bang. The floral heart wreath swayed and fell, wedged between the door and the screen.

CHAPTER THIRTY-SEVEN

My heart was pounding in my chest. I went straight from Emily's to Phil's office. I barely got there before 5:00pm. The secretary rolled her eyes at me. It made me certain why Emily spilled her guts. She thought no one would believe me and she was right. I could have repeated the entire conversation, and I wasn't sure if Kate would believe me. Not with the way things happened. Not with the way the news painted me as some too-simple-minded-to-be-alive type of person. I was still wearing jeans and a tank top, my hair in a messy ponytail, not a stich of make-up on my face.

"Mr. Green will see you now," the receptionist led me to a door.

I was polite, even though part of me wanted to kick her. Phil sat at one end of the table. "Miss Tyndale, finally, you've come to your senses."

I shrugged, and produced the manila envelope, placing it on the table. "I did. He used me. I get it. Fine. Tell him to take this and fuck off. His angel has fallen." Pushing the envelope hard, I sent it sliding toward Phil. He caught it with his hand. The first thing he noticed was the bulge on top. Something was inside, and it wasn't just paper.

Phil looked at me, "What's this?" He looked at Jack's iPhone and pulled out the papers under it. Cocking his head, he sighed, "These aren't signed. Abby..."

"They don't need to be, Phil. Listen to the recording on that phone. And if I were you, I'd do it right now." A sadistic smile spread across my lips. Emily deserved what she had coming. The fierce Abby, the girl I kept locked in a box, was proud. I turned on my heel as Phil started the conversation.

———————

Kate appeared in my doorway. "You saved him, Abby. It's all over the news. That old bitch was arrested, and Jack's name was cleared. Way to work the system. Everyone thought you were too innocent to do something like that. What'd you do, press record and just go knock on her door?"

Nodding, I said, "Something like that. She planned Jack's destruction down to the letter. She didn't care what happened to everyone else. I'm not going to feel guilty about it. She deserves what she gets." Grabbing my coat, I slid it over my shoulders.

"Ah, but you do care. Don't you? And that's why you're running. You can't face Jack."

"Jack's destroyed," I said, wandering around the room. "He'll keep me around out of pity, and I don't want that. Out of sight, out of mind." I stood there, staring at her.

"You're lying to yourself now?" she asked, arms folded over her chest.

"I have to go, Kate." I pushed past her, bags in my hands. "Thank you for putting up with me, but I can't leech off of you anymore." Walking down the hall, I came to an abrupt stop. There was a large package sitting in front of the door. I'd spent the entire day hiding in my room after I got back from Phil's. I packed as fast as possible, but it still took several hours. Eventually Kate noticed, but she failed to mention this.

My heart was in my throat. "What's that?"

Kate stepped around me, tapping the crate, "Something from Jonathan Gray, to Abby Tyndale." She watched me for a second, standing frozen, not knowing what to do. Part of me wanted to open it, part of me wanted to run. "At least look at it, Abby."

Look at it? Look and see what Jack sent me? I wondered if I could do it. It felt like there was no air in the room. I pressed my lips together wondering if it was what I thought it was. Dropping my bags, I walked to the crate. Kate produced pliers and we pulled it apart. Inside was a massive rolled canvas. I glanced at her, but she was already moving, pushing furniture back to make room for it. I placed the canvas on the floor gently, like it was a baby. My heart pounded in my chest, threatening to crack my ribs. I pushed the canvas and it unrolled. Shoulders rigid, I stood there shocked, staring.

Kate gazed over my shoulder, her jaw dropped, "Abby," she gasped. "This is exquisite… It exceeds all his other works combined." She sounded giddy, but I stood there frozen. Staring. Staring at something that might have been, something lost, like a once upon a time story without an ending. I couldn't breathe. Kate looked more closely at it, examining the vivid blue and orange brush strokes. When the painting was created Jack said he wouldn't show my face, but there was a perfect likeness of me, soft and sensual, staring back. Everything about it was perfect. My chest constricted. I felt like I couldn't breathe.

Leaving my bags in the hall, I ran outside. The press was gone. It was just a dark street lined with cars. Kate followed me half a beat later. "What's wrong with you? Abby, talk to me!" She grabbed my arm, turning me back toward her. The sky had finally stopped dropping buckets of rain, but the streets were still damp. They shone like ink.

"I can't look at it, Kate. Get rid of it. Please," I begged her. She looked at me like I was nuts, but nodded. "It's painful... Send it back."

Kate pulled me back inside. Jack had never called me. He never followed up to say thank you for exposing the heinous witch that tried to send me to jail. He never took back his last words to me. He continued to let me think everything we shared was a lie, and the painting reminded me of that. Of him. I couldn't stand it. It felt like I was going to crawl out of my skin. Kate seemed to understand.

She rolled up the goddess version of me and shoved it back in the crate. Taking off the return slip, she turned to me, "Uh, Abby. This can't be returned..."

I sat in a chair, trying to avoid looking at the offending painting until it was out of sight, "Why not?"

"There's a certificate that says the painting is yours. You're the owner. You're supposed to file this slip of the estimated value with your insurance company." She held up a piece of paper.

I held out my hand, "Let me see that." Kate slid the slip between my fingers. It said Abby Tyndale was the owner of AWAKENING by Jonathan Gray, est. value $270,000. I clutched the slip to my chest, like it would revive me if I died. Why was he doing this to me?

Kate sputtered, "Isn't that what you owe on your loans?" I nodded, crumpling the ball in my fist. "Hey! Hey!" Kate ran over and pulled the wrinkled paper from my hands before I shredded it. "Abby, you need that. Take the painting to Southerby's or another auction house and get rid of it if you don't want it—

but don't throw it away." I glanced up at her, "You have that I'm-gonna-shred-stuff look in your eye."

"I won't shred it," I slumped back in my chair. "Call them. Sell it. I'm staying until it's gone." Walking back to the hall, I grabbed my bags and tossed them on my bed.

I could hear Kate's voice as she called the right people in the right places.

CHAPTER THIRTY-EIGHT

A week passed while I waited. Jack fell off the face of the Earth. There was no mention of him in the press. He was just gone like I would be at the end of the week. The auction was Saturday night. Apparently I was lucky and made it just in time to include my painting in with some other big name artists, however Jonathan Gray would have been the biggest name before his scandal.

Kate explained, "It might not sell for much, Abby. It's still very close to the scandal, but they also said there is the small possibility that it'll sell for more than the estimate. Pre-scandal, it would have sold for millions, but now... they just don't know."

Leaning over the kitchen table, I reached for the sugar, dumping a bunch of it into my coffee. I shrugged, "I don't care what it sells for. I just want it gone."

She nodded, "I understand. I just wanted you to know that it might not solve all your problems. The loans may still be there after this, and if they are— you can stay with me, Abby. You don't have to leave."

I smiled at her, mixing my drink, "Thanks, Kate. I really liked having you around, but everywhere I go—I'm afraid I'll see him. I need some space. I need the peace of mind that comes with distance. I wish you could come with me, but I know your life is here. Maybe you can visit once in a while?"

She smiled sadly, "I'd like that. Better go get dressed."

I scoffed, "Why do we have to get dressed up?"

"Because the media will be there and you need to look like a million bucks. Wearing a burlap sack won't mesh with the girl in the painting. Go. Take the little black dress I put on your bed. There's a pair of heels with it. Make yourself look like Holly in Breakfast at Tiffany's." She took my coffee and shoved me out of the kitchen.

CHAPTER THIRTY-NINE

When we arrived at the auction house there was a lot of buzz and hushed whispers. Emily's claims about Jack's work being the first in a post-modern movement of sensual art were true. Since then people debated it on talk shows and it kept coming up in the news. Add to the fact that this was his last painting before the scandal, and that it was different than his other works, and people wanted to attend just to see the famous 'scandal painting,' as they called it.

Kate and I wandered around backstage, looking at items, waiting quietly for them to present my painting. When I'd first seen it that night, my heart sank. It was so beautiful. The auction house had it stretched and framed. The canvas looked perfect—completely perfect. A golden frame, thick and ornate surrounded the painting. AWAKENING was right. That was the perfect title for this piece. It was the day I realized there was more to me than a timid minister, floundering through life. I just wished that I'd learned the lesson in a less painful way.

I was smoothing my black dress, when Kate pulled me to the wing to watch the auction. The auctioneer said, "This is lot number 324, the AWAKENING by Jonathan Gray. It is the last painting created prior to the scandal, and is also known as THE SCANDAL. It is the only piece of work by Gray that is in full color with vibrant hues. Let the bidding begin."

Kate's hand clutched my arm as the bidding quickly soared over $1,000. "This is good," she whispered in my ear, "They were afraid no one would bid, but with this much activity, you might be able to pay off your loans." She squeezed my arm tightly, practically jumping up and down. The bids swiftly soared over $100,000, still climbing wildly. Paddles flew into the air, one after the other, each person wanting to claim a piece of the scandalous Jonathan Gray. Moments later the bids passed $300,000 and Kate and I watched in horrified silence, wondering how high it would go. There were still multiple bidders driving the price higher and higher. The way the lights displayed the artwork, it was difficult to tell who was bidding. There was an elderly couple in the front row. Every time the bid climbed higher, she would tug her husband's arm and his paddle would fly up. She clearly wanted the painting. But there were others too. People I couldn't see, concealed in shadows at the back of the room.

My stomach flipped in my chest as the price flew up. The auctioneer was saying, "A million two. A million four. A million six." After every increase he pointed at someone. He was speaking so fast that I could barely understand him. My eyes had grown large and I was certain I'd stopped breathing, when the auctioneer said, "Two million eight. Going once, going twice..."

A voice rang out, "Seven million two." Kate glanced at me, her eyes wide like big green dinner plates.

The auctioneer seemed startled, but continued, "Seven two going once, twice. Sold to the gentleman for seven million two. Please step forward." Gasps followed as the man from the back of the room walked toward the stage. Murmuring came in cascades, but I already knew who it was.

Jack Gray took long confident strides toward the auctioneer. Several people snapped his picture, as he neared the stage. I stood frozen in the wing, Kate at my side. She whispered in my ear, "I think he just spent his entire fortune on a painting of you."

Eyes wide, I couldn't even nod. I couldn't breathe. When Jack stood in front of the painting, he beamed. His black tux hugged his body perfectly, showcasing every beautiful angle. He posed for a moment before the painting. The press called for me, and I felt Kate's hand on my back pushing me forward. Jack stood on one side of the painting, looking dashingly perfect as I blinked like a deer in the headlights. Did he really spend his entire fortune on this painting? Could he do that? I glanced at him, and his expression softened. Sadness haunted his eyes like it had when I first came back.

He nodded, "Miss Tyndale."

I ignored his formality. Eyes wide, in shock, I asked, "Why? Why would you spend every penny you had on this?" My voice made it sound like the canvas was just a pile of paint, nothing special at all, but Jack thought otherwise.

"Some things are worth it. Sometimes I freeze, Abby. I don't do what I should. I let precious things slip between my fingers." The room was so silent that the only sound I could hear was my heart pounding in my ears. He was speaking of our past, of that kiss that almost happened all those years ago. He was talking about the past few weeks, how he pushed me away, growing increasingly colder. He froze me, utterly chilled my soul, and made me think I was completely wrong about him. But this made no sense. The longing in his eyes, the emptiness that was so visible, made me freeze in place. My knees were stiff, my legs glued to the floor. They felt like they were made of iron and would not bend or move, no matter how much my mind screamed to run and never look back.

"I lost everything, and it was my own damn fault. I thought I was helping you, but I wasn't. I should have seen it. I should have known," he shook his head. His jaw was tight, his eyes filled with regret, "If this is the closest I'll ever get to you again, it was worth it. Every penny." Blinking, I stared at him, pulse pounding in my head. "Say something, Abby."

Silence passed. It felt like hours, but it was only a matter of moments. Finally I shook my head, pressing my lips into a thin line, I said, "I have nothing to say, Jack." He pressed his eyes closed, defeated. Slowly, he started to turn from me. Reaching for him, he stopped, blue eyes meeting mine with a soft worried expression on his face, pain in his eyes. Stepping toward him, I took his face between my hands. Our eyes locked. My body tingled as I touched him, as he gazed at me with those eyes. Our faces moved together, our lips nearly touching, but this time I didn't stop. I didn't wait for Jack. I knew what I wanted and I took it. My lips pressed against his lightly at first. Jack's shock quickly faded as he threw his arms around me, pulling me tightly against his chest. An array of flashes went off as people erupted into chatter.

CHAPTER FORTY

Several weeks later Kate walked down the aisle ahead of me in a plum colored bridesmaid dress with a mammoth bow on her butt and a matching monstrosity on the top of her head. She wore it with grace, as she floated down the aisle of the little clapboard church. I peeked between the doors, watching, my heart fluttering in my chest.

I was wearing an ivory gown adorned with white pearls and lace. It flowed around me like petals on a flower. The bodice hugged me tightly, and laced up in the back. Fabric draped across my shoulders and hundreds of tiny white flowers were woven into my hair.

Leaning back, the wedding planner fanned my train. "Ready, Abby?"

I nodded, beaming at her. The two whitewashed wooden doors slowly opened in front of me as I walked down the aisle to the wedding march. It took every ounce of restraint not to run. The look on Jack's face was a combination of awe and lust. My heart raced faster and I was certain I walked too fast, nearly kicking the photographer out of the way. Smiling broadly, we said our vows, hand in hand.

The minister said, "I now present you with Mr. and Mrs. Gray." Jack and I ran down the aisle and outside to where a car waited to take us away. We grinned, running though the paparazzi, not minding their presence. They repaired Jack's career as fast as they destroyed it over the past few weeks. The auction transferred Jack's entire fortune to me, demonstrating to the world how much he adored me. Since then, the stories came up over and over again—they couldn't believe that they missed it. All those years they spent looking for dirt on Jack were wasted, because they saw that the reason for his solitude was that he was madly in love with me. I was the one that got away, and by the time he found me it was too late. I'd taken my vows and he didn't want to make me fall. Stories appeared calling us the star-crossed lovers that we were.

I dove into the car first, my lacy dress flowing around my ankles. Jack followed, laughing, falling into me. His tuxedo fit him perfectly. The dark charcoal gray made his eyes seem impossibly blue. Giggling, I helped him up, loving the feeling of his hands on my body.

As the driver pulled away, Jack leaned in close. Blue eyes burning, a wicked smile spread across his lips, "I have an idea for a wedding portrait, Mrs. Gray." He kissed my neck, and I melted in his arms.

MORE ROMANCE BOOKS
BY H.M. WARD

SCANDALOUS 2

SECRETS

THE SECRET LIFE OF
TRYSTAN SCOTT

DAMAGED

THE ARRANGEMENT

CAN'T WAIT FOR H.M. WARD'S NEXT STEAMY BOOK?

Let her know by leaving stars and telling her what you liked about SCANDALOUS in an Amazon review!

Made in the USA
Lexington, KY
09 March 2014

Made in the USA
Lexington, KY
09 March 2014